PATSY LEE

A Southern Family

Unexpected Challenges & Changing Fortunes

LARGE PRINT EDITION

Book Cover & Interior Layout © 2022 Harvest Creek Publishing & Design

Harvest Creek Publishing & Design
12050 White Oak Ranch Drive
Conroe, TX 77304
www.harvestcreek.net

A Southern Family. — 1st ed.
ISBN 978-1-7373567-9-0

Printed in The United States of America

I want to dedicate this book to my twin daughters, who have been the joy of my life, and to thank them for the unbounding love we share. A special thanks for their superb editing, without which this book would be full of unnecessary semi-colons and neglect of compound words.

A
Southern
Family

Elisabeth
Chambers

Martha Dalton	Lydia Dalton	James Dalton
Married Elbert Hall	Married Walter Wiggins	Married Sally Ann Johnston

Mattie Hall

Wyatt Dalton

Mason Hall

Willard Dalton

Eliza Hall

The Dalton Family Tree

John
Dalton

| Tabitha Dalton | Rachel Dalton | Abigail Dalton |
| Married Leeland Collins | Married Frederick Hall | Married Dirk Dunaway, then Doug Dunaway |

Jack Dunaway

Robert Dunaway

Other Dalton Family Siblings:
- *Helena Dalton*
- *Phoebe Dalton*
- *Miriam Dalton*
- *Andrew Dalton*
- *Henry Dalton*

CHAPTER 1

MARTHA AND THE FARM

The loud crack of the slamming back door made Martha look up from hanging sheets on the clothesline. Two little sisters bolted across the screened porch like bank robbers making their getaway. In the lead was six-year-old Abigail whooping it up with eight-year-old Rachel, trying to catch her by the sash. As they headed down the steps, Martha heard them squabbling.

"Hush, Abigail. You gonna wake the baby," Rachel chastised.

"You're not the boss of me." Abigail headed for the pig pen where the new piglets were. Her dash had caused the chickens roaming the yard to run like tails afire, and they set up an angry squawk.

Martha turned back to her laundry and took a moment to feel the gusty breeze ruffle her hair. She loved the smell of fresh laundry and marveled at nature as she watched the sheets billow like birds trying to take flight. The clothes would be dry by mid-afternoon. Monday was wash day, and there was a busy day ahead. Now that school was out, Martha had organized and assigned chores to her younger sisters to keep them engaged and out of mischief. Unfortunately, Mama was busy with the new baby and had not regained her strength.

"Rachel, you head on over to the henhouse now. Gather the eggs," Martha called out as she returned to the house and set the laundry basket on the back porch. She picked up the vegetable basket and headed to the garden to pick beans. Any work in the garden was best done before it got too hot. Life never slowed down.

After picking enough beans for the large crowd at dinner, Martha headed to the wrap-around porch. It was peaceful here, and she looked forward to a bit of time to herself. It was the place where every Sunday, after church and dinner, the family and other kinfolk gathered. While the kids and their cousins played in the front yard, the grown-ups would sit and rock, catch up on the community gossip, and watch the world go by on this dusty highway. Although the farm was a bucolic place, it didn't suit her. She remembered arguing with her brother, James.

"I want me a house in town, one of those white-washed ones."

"Not me," James had replied. "I like this old, weathered clapboard. Feels homey. And in town, you don't have room for all these trees surrounding the house, providing cool shade and places for the birds to sing their hearts out in the evening." James was dreamy-eyed.

"In town, you don't have these endless farm chores." Martha thought that would win the argument.

"Got to keep up the chores for the farm to be prosperous. I love a house in the middle of big acreage and lots of woods nearby. The ideal place to raise a family just like other country folk."

"One day, all this will be yours, James. The oldest boy and only son," Martha said without a trace of jealousy.

She recalled this conversation as the rhythm of snapping beans created a mind lull. Everyone had their place, and she and her sisters would someday marry and leave this place. She felt responsible for keeping order among the family chaos. Aunt Dolly had told her she had an independent spirit and was a natural at being in charge. She was willing to work hard at something she liked. Although she didn't see her way clearly, she knew she did not want to end up like poor Mama, with one child right after the other. And Papa, whom she loved dearly, struggled so hard to make ends meet on this farm.

She took the bowl of beans and went back around to the kitchen. Just then, James emerged from the barn with a large wrench.

"Having trouble with old Matilda this morning," he said as he headed for the second-hand tractor and wiped a bead of sweat off his forehead with his shirtsleeve. Martha felt sorry for him; he was only 14 years old but had to carry a lot of weight for the farm work.

"Giving you a hard time, is she?" Martha said.

"That's all right. I'd rather be doing this than sitting in that darn fool schoolroom learning worthless stuff."

"Oh, James, you know school is good for you." She liked to tease him.

"Easy for you to say. You only have one more year."

In a few minutes, she heard the sputtering and putt-putt as the tractor came to life. James climbed aboard and headed for the fields. Then, she heard him call out, "Better go. I see Louis waiting on me down yonder."

Martha saw Louis waving at James. Those two were best friends, both of them being the only boys in families of girls. Louis lived on a farm down the road, and he and his daddy helped out from time to time, just like good neighbors do for each other. Martha knew when the work was done, James and Louis would scurry down to the creek and come back with a mess of fish.

"Yes, and I'd better get these beans on the stove," she muttered to herself. The family had their dinner, the largest meal, at noon because the menfolk, including her brother, father, and the hired hands, had been working since sunup and would be at it all afternoon until sunset. There were a lot of chores to be done before dinner time, and they came in hungry as bears. Supper time would be more relaxed with the leftovers from dinner.

CHAPTER 2

MARTHA AND THE STORE

Among Martha's chores was the responsibility for the country store that Papa had set up about two years ago in the south corner of the farm to supplement the income for the needs of their growing family. The store was stocked with the staples needed by neighbors in the community and items desired by thirsty travelers coming down the road from as far away as Atlanta. Later that afternoon, after taking in the laundry, Martha headed to the store to relieve her sister Lydia, who had the early afternoon shift. The travelers would be coming through as the sun went down.

"What you need to learn about merchandising, Martha," Papa had said, "is to have handy the things people want as well as things to tempt them with, things they didn't even know they wanted." She found out that cold drinks, sardines, potted meat and saltines sold well at dinner time.

By afternoon, people passing through wanted cold drinks, a bag of chitlins, or salted peanuts. Those that came late afternoon wanted fresh vegetables and meat for supper. Tabitha, Martha's twelve-year-old sister, didn't like it, but her job was to wring the chickens' necks and dress them in time for the afternoon shoppers. Any that didn't sell by the time the store closed became chicken and dumplings for the Dalton family the next day.

"You need to ask the customers if they want some smoked ham and sausage for breakfast while they are shopping." Papa was ever the salesman. He was always thinking ahead, anticipating what people needed. He had recently put in a gas tank because there were more and more cars along the highway.

"These ole dirt farmers don't have a prayer of ever owning a car, but they stop by out of curiosity to see the horseless carriages. That's a good thing because they end up buying something in the store like that's what they came for in the first place."

Because she kept the books, Martha knew the income from the store was a good part of the farm's livelihood. It was located on the edge of the highway, with a sign you couldn't miss, "Dalton General Store," Martha's favorite place on the farm. She had helped Papa plan how the store was organized.

It was essentially one big room where the merchandise was laid out in rows. There was a small office and storeroom in the back. The two front steps led up to a shaded porch where the icebox full of sodas stood so customers could help themselves and then pay inside. Papa had put some chairs on the front porch so folks could sit for a while and exchange gossip.

Just last week, she had heard two people on the porch talking. "Did you hear about Tom and Bertie's girl? Ran off with that Simmons boy. Heard they went to Alabama. Know it broke Bertie's heart."

When Martha entered the store, she smelled the loose tobacco in the cloth pouches that sold so well. Although Lydia had probably had a quiet day and been reading most of the time, Martha knew she would be glad she could leave.

Martha slowly shook her head at the produce display Lydia had set up. Unfortunately, the watermelons were in the front, blocking the view of the beans and squash! How often had Papa told them, "If you are going to do something, do it right?"

She opened the cash register, found a couple of nickels in the penny tray, and moved them. Then she muttered, "At fifteen, Lydia should not be so careless." She knew she would be wasting her breath to criticize her though. Usually, Lydia was anxious to leave, so Martha was surprised to see her lingering near the front of the store and looking out the window.

She heard heavy boot steps on the porch, and the screen door opened. In came a burly looking man covered with the red dust of Georgia and at least two days' beard growth. Martha saw that he had gotten a Nehi Orange out of the icebox and was surveying the wares at the front of the store where Lydia was.

She heard Lydia say, "May I help you, sir? Oh my, you have the bluest eyes I have ever seen!" Martha frowned and sensed trouble. The girl was a shameless flirt.

"You are a mighty pretty young lady—a sight for these sore blue eyes." He had a raspy voice and had moved closer to her.

"Why, thank you, sir. My name is Lydia. What's yours?"

"I'm Clyde Taylor, Ma'am," he said, taking off his wide-brimmed hat. He pulled out some coins to pay for his drink. Lydia took the money ever so slowly as she continued to smile at him.

"Ooh, what's that scar on your face? How did you get that?"

"Lydia!" Martha called out as she walked toward them and looked out the window to see the man's horse at the watering trough.

"Lydia, put the money in the right trays. And your shift at the store is over, so go on to the barn. It's milking time."

Martha sensed that Mr. Taylor felt the tension and left the store to wait outside.

CHAPTER 3

LYDIA–MILKING & DAYDREAMING

Lydia was humiliated, having Martha give her instructions. "I guess Mr. Blue Eyes thinks I'm just a milkmaid," she mumbled. She grabbed her book from the counter as she went out to clang the bell. The afternoon milking was another of her daily jobs. Thank goodness it wasn't the first thing in the morning. James had to do that. She hated nothing more than getting up at the crack of dawn.

Lydia loathed farm life with the incessant chores and the rigid schedule of things that had to be done at the same time of day, over and over again, seven days a week. Fortunately, milking was her least despised job. She strolled out to the barn and got the milking stool. She hated the rancid smell of the cow barn and was careful where she stepped.

"Well, Elsie, I see you've been eating well. Your bag is full, just like yesterday." During milking time, she thought about the rhythm of life. That udder filled up every morning and every night. Just like the sun and the moon. Just like the stars that came out every night.

"Oops, you thought I wasn't paying attention, didn't you, Elsie, swishing that dirty ole tail at me. And don't you dare try kicking over the milk bucket." Then, with a few precautions, she was free to let her mind wander while she performed the repetitious task of pulling and squeezing.

Lydia liked to daydream as much as she liked to read. Grandpa Chambers had called her his little philosopher because she borrowed those kinds of books from his library. Lydia was now reading *Pragmatism* by William James. She considered herself a pragmatist. She thought the best way to get what you wanted out of life was to be practical.

Just today, she read, "The art of being wise is the art of knowing what to overlook." She knew what to overlook—lots of things around this farm. Martha didn't overlook anything and spent too much time ensuring everything was just right. But what difference did it make in the long run? You just wasted time and energy doing things that had to be done again. Take dusting the furniture, for example; you dusted one day, but the dust was right back the next day. Just be practical and let it be.

Oh, she knew there were lots of farm chores that had to be done. And she understood Mama and Papa's philosophy that every family member had to do their share. But it wasn't *practical* to force people to do jobs they didn't like.

Take Tabitha, for instance. Just because Tabitha was twelve years old didn't mean she should have to wring the chicken's neck for the store supply. Tabitha—who hated the sight of blood! The practical thing would be to figure out what people are good at and let them do that.

Maybe Tabitha could learn to bake pies to sell at the store. Then she would be *eager* instead of dreading her daily job. And she might be in a better mood instead of always being crabby. Mama usually criticized the job she was doing, picking off the feathers. Lydia had heard Tabitha mumble, "I guess I never do anything right." Yes, siree, pragmatism could teach this family a lot!

Something Lydia had read struck a chord with her. *To change one's life: Start immediately. Do it flamboyantly. No exceptions.*

She would copy this down in the journal she wrote in every night. Then, she would do it with a big splash when she was ready to act.

She looked forward to evenings when she always read something lighter than philosophy. She was currently reading *Riders of the Purple Sage*. The gunslinger fought the savages and saved a beautiful young woman from marrying against her will— what a romantic adventure! She sighed as she closed her eyes, kept milking, and daydreamed of the blue-eyed stranger.

CHAPTER 4

MARTHA AND THE MERCHANT

With Lydia gone, Martha rearranged the produce, humming as she worked. Lydia had left the morning's eggs in the basket under the counter, and Martha moved them into the blue speckled enamel bowl next to the cash register. She moved the beef and pork from the smokehouse to a more prominent place.

The store's appeal for her was the orderliness, the exactness of the books, and the neatly sorted money. She had a talent for adding up the costs and making the correct change, and Papa trusted her. Unlike Lydia, who showed no ambition and made all sorts of excuses for doing the least amount of work in the house or in the yard, Martha liked staying busy. She preferred helping Papa with the business of the farm over doing housework.

Martha heard it before she saw it. A big, black, shiny car pulled into the drive near the gas pump. She clanged the bell for Papa and watched the well-dressed gentleman as he came into the store. He took his time looking around but didn't seem to be interested in buying any produce. Instead, he kept eyeing Martha to the point of making her nervous.

"Sure am glad to be back home. Atlanta's traffic, people and noise are enough to drive a man insane."

"Is there anything I can help you find?"

"I just need some gas."

"Yes, I've rung for Papa. He will be here in a few minutes."

"I'll take one of these watermelons. Pick me out a good one, will you?"

As she came from behind the counter, she could feel his eyes on her.

"Hey, I'd guess you are a size 8; I've got a dandy dress in the car that I bet would just fit you."

Martha stopped thumping the watermelon and said, "Whaaat?"

"Oh, I guess you don't know that I'm Sam Crawford, and I have the department store on the corner of Jackson and Forrest Streets in town. I've been to Atlanta on a buying trip for the latest fashions. Getting new merchandise in time for Fall. The hem lengths are getting shorter, showing more of the legs." Martha felt herself blushing as he glanced at her legs.

"Say, with your coloring, a red dress would be very flattering."

Unconsciously, Martha smoothed her hair. He had piqued her curiosity, but so as not to encourage him, she responded, "Mama makes all our dresses; she gets her ideas from the Sears and Roebuck catalog."

"Well, you drop in my store the next time you are in town and have a look at my dresses. I am hiring girls like you as sales clerks." He took the watermelon she held and walked back outside.

She knew Papa would have heard the bell and seen the car drive up and would have come to pump gas for this man. She moved closer to the window and heard Papa's voice in a lively conversation with his customer. He was always eager to hear news of Atlanta and events that might affect the farming business.

Martha studied the gentleman. Next to Papa, he looked short and thin but had an air about him that suggested self-confidence. His black hair was slicked back, no doubt with pomade. She could see he was talkative; well, after all, he was a salesman. She looked down at her faded blue gingham dress. Could she ever see herself working in a department store? Red? She never wore red. She watched him pull out his wallet and pay Papa, then get back in his car and drive away. She felt a curious mixture of attraction to what he promised and anxiety at the thought of venturing beyond her secure world.

After the day's chores were done and Martha had locked up the store, she joined the family for supper. Everyone had their place at the long table: Papa at the head, Mama at the foot, and Miriam on the corner in the bassinet. The older children sat on Papa's right: Martha, Lydia, James and Tabitha. In stair-step order, Rachel, Abigail, Helena and Phoebe were on the other side.

Everyone bowed their heads while Papa blessed the food and said, "Amen." Mama was a good cook. The cold fried chicken and sweet potatoes were good. Deviled eggs and green beans rounded out the meal. The Apple Brown Betty was just as good tonight as it had been at dinner time.

It was Lydia and Rachel's turn to wash and dry the dishes. Martha stood, ready to help Mama put the little ones to bed. James announced he was meeting Louis to go catch lightning bugs. Everything was settling into place when Martha noticed Mama wince as Papa headed out the back door and to the barn. She heard Mama mumble, "Oh, no, John, not again."

CHAPTER 5

JAMES IS PAPA'S KEEPER

James was always the one to find him late at night when it happened. He was coming into the barn with his jar of lightning bugs that he and Louis had caught when he heard the snoring inside one of the stalls. Papa was passed out on a straw bed—the whiskey bottle beside him. He smelled worse than a polecat.

James decided to leave him where he was and to cover him with the old blanket they kept in the barn. Mama acted like she didn't know. At least he could keep the younger kids from knowing their daddy had a weakness that frequently reduced him to this embarrassing state. James swore he would never touch the first drop, not if this was what it led to. What in the devil did anyone get out of acting like a fool?

Although James couldn't understand it, he believed Papa tried to resist. The barn was his place to pray, to fight the temptation. Yet he kept that bottle hidden there. Kind of a test of his courage to see if he could resist when it was in plain sight. But why would you keep tempting yourself if you failed the test repeatedly?

James had confided in no one about what his daddy did from time to time. No one except Sally Ann. She was a sweet thing and would listen to him and understand his agony and his helplessness. Her daddy drank too, and not just occasionally, according to her. Sally Ann would hold James' hand and say he was so brave to take care of his dad and keep the family secret from all those who thought John Dalton was such an upstanding citizen. Uncle Gene knew about it; he was the one who had first called James when it required two strong men to get John home and into the barn to sleep it off.

"Son, there are some things we just don't understand. Your papa worries about the farm and gets overwhelmed with the challenges. He doesn't want to be a failure and prove Bett's father right."

"What do you mean?" James asked.

"When you are old enough, I'll explain, James. But remember, your father is a good man, but he can't resist the bottle. He tries; Lord knows he does. We have to keep this from the womenfolk. One day, John will conquer this. I know he will. It could be worse. There are all sorts of other temptations in this world."

"Yes, sir," was all James could think of to say. He wondered what Uncle Gene meant. James couldn't think of any worse temptations. He would find out soon enough.

CHAPTER 6

JAMES AND THE CHURCH

James had grown taller over the last few years, although he still was not quite as tall as his father, who stood at the front of the church leading the singing. Sitting on the pew with his sisters, he was lost in private thought. He felt lonely most of the time, being the only boy in the family. What he loved was to be outdoors, with or without company.

He was proud to be Papa's partner for the tough jobs, like cutting the timber and hauling logs to the sawmill. He could handle the animals, too. Farm life was for him, and he knew when he was old enough, Papa would give him some land of his own. He was content with the life of a farmer, with its steady pace of chores for each season. Ever since James was a young boy, he had been doing the work of a man, and he had the muscles to prove it.

He knew he and Martha had nothing in common except being hard workers. He was quiet like Martha but didn't share her interest in school, and he sure didn't keep his nose in a book like Lydia. Instead, he learned all he needed to know from watching the cycle of life on the farm and seeing the rhythm of people in their small community.

Mama kept having girls; she wanted them to be "Southern ladies" and would not allow Papa to ask them to do hard work outside. So James was the only one to help Papa with the never-ending work. He could see Papa was exhausted most evenings when he came in for the night. So was he, especially when he had chores before and after school.

Anyway, he would finish the eleventh grade this coming year and be done with school forever. Papa had told him that he would always have a home at the farm. When he was old enough, he would get some acreage of his own and could build a separate house. But how could Papa manage then? Sure, the neighbors helped each other, and he could count on Louis' dad, but there were the daily chores. His sisters were no good on the farm; they just had easy jobs and hated doing even those. Mama was too easy on them.

Church was a big part of family life, but the thing James liked best about Sunday was he got to rest, except for the few chores that had to be done. Sitting and listening to the preacher seemed useless to him. Everyone just went home and committed sin all week until the following Sunday. Mama and Papa loved to sing, and he had to admit that was pleasant.

He had not been blessed with a singing voice or the ability to play musical instruments, although Mama had tried to teach him. When people in the congregation responded "Amen" to the preaching, he felt they were just trying to show off or pretend to be paying close attention.

Sally Ann, the girl at school he liked, never came to church, and neither did her family. She probably didn't have parents who insisted that going to church was the only way to Heaven. He imagined she got to sleep late, went on picnics, and maybe even took a swim instead of spending all day in church.

All these thoughts went through James' head, but he kept his face blank and tried to be patient while the time passed, the lengthy sermon was over, and the last song had been sung.

CHAPTER 7

LYDIA & WALTER

Tall, dark and handsome. That's how she would describe him. Well, maybe a touch of gray, but still very handsome. She was glad she had curled her hair on the rag rollers last night. It was shiny and fluffy today. She gave him a big smile.

"My pretty Lydia! So glad it is you in the store today!"

"Well, I don't know why you are so surprised. I'm the best one at keeping the store in order."

He was flirty, and she was flirty right back. She knew Walter lived in Florida and that he traveled back and forth from Atlanta about every two weeks. He had offered to give her a ride in his big car, but Mama had had a fit at the idea.

"What would the neighbors think?" That was always Mama's concern—the appearance of things. But this particular day was so pretty, and spring was in the air. What harm would a little ole ride do? On an impulse, she agreed this time. "I would love to, as

long as it is just to Hammond's Crossing and back."
The store would be all right for that few minutes, and
Mama was probably busy in the house with Andrew,
the new baby. She need never know.

As Walter helped Lydia into the car, she felt a thrill
like never before. What if she was on her way to
Florida? What a delicious feeling that would be! He
was true to his word and turned around and got her
back to the store before anyone noticed. Or had they?
Well, what if they had? She was nearly a grown woman
now, right? She didn't have many opportunities to
meet gentlemen. There were only rowdy redneck boys
at church. At the movies on Saturday, it was the same
thing. Tobacco-chewing hicks.

Walter saw her safely back in the store and bought
an RC cola and a bag of salted peanuts. As he
prepared to leave, Lydia reached up, kissed him on
the cheek, and thanked him for the ride. "That was
the most fun I've had in a long time," she smiled and
batted her eyes at him, the way she had seen in the
picture shows in town. As Lydia watched Walter
drive off down the road, she had a deep longing
tinged with fear that life was passing her by. Her
indignation kicked in, and she knew it was up to her
to shape her own future.

That night, with her imagination fired up, she wrote
a captivating story in her journal. Martha would
come into the store to relieve her and find everything
eerily quiet with no Lydia in sight. The whole family

would be in an uproar, searching for her. James would come in from the field and shock everyone by saying he saw a man alone drive up to the store in a big shiny car but saw two people in the car speeding down the road a few minutes later.

CHAPTER 8

LYDIA EAVESDROPS

L ydia curled up in the big easy chair in the living room to be all by herself and read. The window was open, and she felt a slight breeze. Mama and Aunt Dolly were on the front porch, and the drone of their voices and occasional laughter was not a distraction. She had learned to concentrate on reading because complete solitude was rare in this big family.

"Nothing is more peaceful than sitting and rocking a baby, so soft and sweet. We both could fall asleep." Mama laughed in her mirthful way.

Lydia heard Aunt Dolly say, "Sis, did you ever think you would end up like this, working so hard? We didn't know how lucky we were growing up in the parsonage, wearing pretty clothes all the time. The hardest chore was visiting the old biddies Mama showed Christian charity to." Lydia heard them both laughing at the memories. Then, she started paying attention because she always loved hearing stories about Mama growing up in town at the parsonage. It had seemed like a charmed life to Lydia, and she never tired of hearing the romantic story of her parents.

"I know I shocked everyone when John and I started courting," Mama said. Lydia sat up. *Why was that a shock?* She had never heard that before.

Aunt Dolly mocked the ladies of the church in a high-pitched voice. "What can she be thinking? A girl like that raised with all the privileges of a well-to-do family. The daughter of a prominent citizen of the town, sheltered from the harsh realities of life and brought up to be a lady of leisure! Sweethearts with a farmer."

Lydia frowned as she listened for more.

"But the first time that tall, handsome, and gentled-faced John smiled at me, I was smitten," Mama said.

What she heard next almost made her gasp out loud. Aunt Dolly was saying, "Remember that fateful day that John asked Daddy for your hand in marriage? I thought Daddy would have a stroke. He had planned on you marrying that circuit-rider preacher." Dolly used her deep masculine voice this time. "Indeed, daughter of the Reverend Doctor James Henry Chambers, the best-educated man in the county, highly respected and admired, marrying a poor, uneducated dirt farmer!"

Lydia felt hurt on Mama's behalf. Grandpa Chambers said that! She had had no idea.

Mama sounded defiant. "John was a farmer, but I loved him. After all, he was from a prosperous, well-respected family. Just look at the vast amount of farmland and woods on our property. We won't do that to our children. John has always said he wanted his children to choose whom *they* wanted to marry. Then he would give his blessing, not his permission."

"I know John will give his children that freedom, but I know you, Elizabeth Ann Dalton. You are enough like our daddy. You will do everything you can to steer your children to a choice that has your approval." Lydia nodded her head in agreement as she remained silent.

"Mama and Daddy thought I would have made a good preacher's wife because I can play the piano and organ. But you see, I can play it just as well being a farmer's wife, and John has such a good singing voice." Lydia had never heard Mama talk like this, as if she needed to prove herself.

"How do you manage all these children, Betts?"

"The kids all have chores, and the older ones help look after the younger ones," Betts said.

"Well, when you have so many kids, I don't see how you can possibly give each one individual attention, meet their needs," Dolly said as she watched the busy brood running to and fro in the yard.

"Oh, I take care of each one of my children, Dolly. I could always see about things better than you," Betts laughed. Lydia had noticed the competition between these two sisters whenever they got together. Aunt Dolly tried to be the boss as the older sister. Just like with Martha and me, Lydia thought.

"John and I are very happy. Of course, we both have our faults, but I dare say everyone does, even that preacher I didn't marry."

They were quiet for a while, and Lydia returned to her reading. She was just getting into it when she heard Mama say, "Well, Dolly, I guess I might as well tell you, there's another little one on the way. We keep hoping for another boy this time, but we will take whatever the good Lord sends, and as long as He sends them."

"Oh, Betts, maybe you need to tell the Lord that after this one, your body needs a rest. After all, you are over 40 years old now. Martha may be getting married soon, and you may start having grandbabies." Betts just laughed and kept rocking little Andrew in her lap.

Lydia jolted when she heard a masculine voice. She must have fallen asleep still curled up in her chair. Her book lay open on her lap. She realized Aunt Dolly and Uncle Gene must have left, and Papa had joined Mama on the porch.

"John, I've been thinking about Martha. It's time she thought about finding a husband. I respect your wish to let the children choose their own mate, but I think that young preacher would be ideal. Martha is a good soul, just the kind of partner a preacher needs. Of course, she doesn't have any musical talent that would be an asset to a preacher. Still, she could express her ministry in another way and be just as much a helpmate."

So that was why Mama had invited Reverend Josh home several times for Sunday dinner! Lydia knew about romance from the books she read, and she didn't see any interest on his part or Martha's. In fact, he didn't express interest in any girl in the congregation. She knew Mama wanted a preacher in the family. Lydia wondered if that made Papa think she wished she had married a preacher instead of him. James would never make a preacher.

Lydia could see that of all the girls, Martha was best suited for a life in the parsonage. But that sure wasn't the life she wanted—it would be a lot of work. She pondered each of her sisters in that role. Rachel, Tabitha and Helena were all too shy; Abigail was too wild, as was Phoebe. Miriam was too young to tell. No, it would have to be Martha.

She heard Mama say, "I might have to sit her down and talk heart-to-heart with Martha. If parents don't push these things, the children will end up matched with the wrong kind of person."

Papa sighed. "Let me talk to her. I'll do it next time that it is just the two of us at the store." Mama's words reverberated in Lydia's ears... *matched with the wrong kind of person.*

"I hope all our children will live close by and stay connected as a family," Lydia heard Mama say. "The farm property is large and can be parceled out. If the girls married someone from the community, someone whose family had been here for generations, they would all be close by. And as we get older, they would be nearby to see us through old age."

"Times are changing, Betts. I'm not sure we can keep them down on the farm."

You are so right, Papa, Lydia thought. *But isn't that selfish of Mama? Doesn't she want her children to have their own lives? Discover the big, wide world? Or am I the one being selfish? If I am, then why do I dislike the idea of living close by on a farm?*

CHAPTER 9

ABIGAIL AND HER HAIR

Mama, will you braid my hair?" pleaded Abigail. She couldn't stand it to flop over her face. It needed cutting anyway. "Wearing it down makes my neck sweaty," said Abigail.

Mama was scurrying around cleaning up the kitchen after breakfast and didn't answer her. Abigail repeated her question, this time with more urgency.

"Child, I don't have time to braid your hair. Don't you see how busy I am? I got canning to do today, and then I'm making watermelon rind preserves. Get one of your sisters to do it." Abigail could hear the tiredness in her mother's voice.

"Lydia and Tabitha don't do it tight enough, and it starts to fall out."

"Well, maybe you shouldn't be so persnickety, Miss Priss." Abigail noticed that Mama's own hair was up in a tight bun, held in place with bobby pins. Mama always looked put together, more like a preacher's wife than a farmer's.

"Mama, please, it will only take five minutes," Abigail begged.

"Young lady, you are about to get on my bad side. Your hair is the least important thing I have to do this morning."

Abigail knew that tone and bounded out of the house, letting the door slam a little too hard. She wanted Mama to know she was mad too. She moved too fast to get a swat on the backside for sassing.

It was already getting warm outside, and there was no breeze whatsoever. Ugh, this thick hair would be her nemesis today. With rawhide bands in hand, Abigail walked down to the store where she knew Martha had gone early that morning to work on the account books for Papa. She would try her luck with her older sister.

"Hey, Pumpkin. Why the long face?" Martha asked as Abigail plopped down beside her.

"Oh, I wanted Mama to take just five minutes and braid my hair, but she doesn't have time for me. She never has time for me."

"And she doesn't even have time for herself either." Martha was always the peacemaker, Abigail knew. She was also what the Bible called "good." She never spoke ill of anyone. But Abigail wasn't sure she had it in her to be like Martha. It would take a lot of work.

"Here, come here; I can braid your hair." Abigail smiled and turned her back so Martha could reach her better.

"You are eight years old—that's old enough to start braiding your own hair," Martha's voice was soothing.

"I can braid. I just can't start it high up." In truth, Abigail liked the hypnotic motion of someone pulling three strands of hair, going in and out, over and across. She closed her eyes and enjoyed the moment. When Martha finished, the braids were nice and tight, just the way Abigail liked them.

"Why is my hair a different color than yours, Martha?" Abigail said to change the subject and prolong their time together.

"Well, I have dark hair like Papa's and his English relatives, and you have strawberry-blonde like Mama's and her Irish relatives. Have you noticed how some of us children have one and some the other? And Papa's folks are all tall, but so far, all of us seem to be average height. The one thing we all got from Mama and Papa is a good name, and we don't want to ever do anything that would disgrace the family."

She didn't want to get into a talk about good behavior, especially since she had just sassed Mama. Instead, she thanked Martha and gave her a kiss on the cheek.

"Well, I'd better go, so you can finish Papa's books."

As Abigail was starting to leave, Martha said, "Since I did something nice for you, why don't you do something nice for me?"

Abigail hesitated and felt puzzled. "What can I do for you?"

"See all those cans on the shelf over there? Turn them so the labels are all facing the front. The customers can see them better, and that affects sales. And it just looks more orderly."

As she began this chore, Abigail thought, *This will take more than five minutes.*

When she came in for dinner, Abigail could tell that Mama noticed her hair but didn't say anything until they were doing the dishes.

"Well, Miss Priss, I see you got someone to braid your hair. You better learn to manage it yourself."

Abigail was fuming but knew better than to sass Mama this time. *I'll show her I'll manage my hair,* Abigail thought. So after the dishes were dried and put away and everyone left the kitchen, Abigail got the shears and whacked off her braids. That ought to make Mama sorry.

She marched into the sitting room. "Now I can manage my hair," she said, expecting looks of horror. But instead, Mama started laughing.

She felt deflated when Mama said, "Well, look what Miss Abigail, the trendsetter, has done! Let's do this for all the girls."

Chapter 10

MARTHA'S FUTURE PLANS

Martha was closing up the store and counting the money for the day when Papa came in. She could tell by the solemn expression on his face that the visit had a purpose.

"Good day, Martha? You made the order for what needs replenishing?"

"Yes to both questions, Papa," she said as she prepared to lock up for the night.

"Before we leave, I want to talk to you for a minute," said Papa with all seriousness. Martha braced herself for what she suspected was to come.

"That preacher man seems sweet on you, baby. What do you think of him?" She knew Papa didn't beat around the bush and expected her to be forthright and tell him the truth.

"He doesn't appeal to me. Too squishy."

"Squishy?" Papa grinned. "That doesn't sound like a fatal error."

"Just too—you know, not very solid. He's too eager to please others. I can't determine who he is and what he stands for."

She saw him consider her words as he searched for some way to salvage his agenda. "Maybe he's trying to live out, 'love thy neighbor.' I think he'd make a nice husband for you. It would surely please your Mama—a preacher in the family once again. James isn't going to fulfill her wish. None of the other girls have the disposition or the...." Papa hesitated then continued, "the... abilities a preacher's wife would need. Your Mama's kinda got her heart set on you and that preacher. You'll be finishing school at the end of this year. You'd have a good life being the mate of a preacher man."

Martha looked him in the eye and was silent for a long minute. "You and Mama married for love, and when and if I marry, I'd like that to be the reason."

Papa sighed. "I can't argue with that." She could see he was coming around.

"Papa, I just don't feel any sparks around Pastor Josh. I get more pleasure out of managing this store than I do out of being in his company."

Papa frowned; Martha knew he was dreading telling Mama. One of the reasons she loved Papa so much was that he was too softhearted to persuade her to do something that would make her unhappy. On the other hand, Martha knew that Mama would think she knew best and that Martha would one day thank her if she married the preacher.

She saw Papa turn to leave as if the conversation were finished. Martha spoke up, "What I'd really like to do is work in Mr. Crawford's store in town."

Papa quickly responded, "I don't think your Mama would allow that." She wasn't surprised, and she was ready.

"Well then, I'd like to go to the college in town. Take some courses, maybe studying teaching." The local college was only two years. After that, some students transferred to senior colleges or universities in the state. Martha did not dare dream of going beyond the two years. She could get a teacher's certificate with that, but she hoped to take some courses in the business school during her stay.

Papa and Martha were both quiet as her expressed desire settled in.

Finally, Papa said, "Well, I guess you could take some courses and still run the store. See how it goes."

"I thought it would be best if I lived in town. Maybe rent a room from cousin Manda."

"But who would manage the store? I don't think Lydia could do it."

"No, and I don't think she could manage the books. And I don't think Tabitha could handle it. But, on the other hand, Abigail seems to have a knack for numbers. Maybe I could train her. She's bold enough to be a good salesman." They both laughed.

Chapter 11

MARTHA MEETS ELBERT

I t was in Psychology class when she noticed him smiling at her. When they left the class, he caught up with her.

"Since we both have an hour before our English class, do you want to go to the Union and have a coke, Martha?" he asked. They knew each other's names because the psychology professor called on students in class.

"I had planned to go to the library and study," Martha replied.

"You can always study, but you can't always have a coke with me." He grinned.

"Oh, okay," she said against her better judgment. She had determined nothing would sidetrack her from getting an education. Why had she given in so easily? Well, he was cute, and she knew from class he was smart.

He steered her to a table in the corner, away from the jukebox.

"You want something to eat? Maybe a hamburger?"

"No, just a coke." She would love a hamburger, but that seemed like asking too much when the offer was for just a coke. She watched him as he went up to the counter. He wasn't very tall, a little stocky, but he had an air of confidence about him. He had blond hair and the kind of eyes that looked at you sincerely. His face was round or appeared that way because he grinned a lot. That usually means a pleasant personality, she thought.

The Union served coke in a frosty glass with Coca-Cola embossed on the side. She knew there was a Coca-Cola bottling company in town, and the main headquarters was in Atlanta. Everybody drank Coca-Cola. She sipped through the straw.

"Very nice and cold. Thank you, Elbert."

"You are so welcome. Do you like the music that is playing? I've got a quarter; tell me what you'd like to hear."

"Oh, you choose. I'm not particular."

When he returned from the jukebox, he surprised her by saying, "Well, tell me about your journey."

"My journey?"

"Yes, your life. Where were you before you came to college, how did you get here, where are you going after?"

"Oh, you want my life history, do you? Okay. I grew up on a farm outside of town. I am the oldest of nine siblings. I'm studying to be a teacher, but what I really like is working in a store. That's about it."

"Nice. I grew up on a farm too. I have one brother —younger. He loves farming, but it's not for me. I want to own a grocery store in town. So I'm working at the Piggly Wiggly now to learn all I can about how to run a grocery store."

So that's why he has so much spending money, Martha thought. "I ran our family general store on the farm. I loved it," Martha said to keep the conversation going.

"I bet you could teach me a lot."

Now, how did he mean that? Martha wondered. She sipped her coke and didn't respond.

"Are you going to the basketball game tonight?" he asked.

"No, I'm staying with my cousin, and she picks me up every day at 5 when she gets off work." She almost said, "And I don't have a way to get back," but she thought that would be like hinting at a ride.

"I live in the dorm and have a car. Why don't I come to pick you up? I'll get you right back home after the game. Just give me directions to your cousin's house."

It was too nice an offer to refuse, and it felt good to have someone doing things for her. She was used to being the one in charge, and it was a new but pleasant feeling to have someone set up the plans and do thoughtful things for her.

Elbert took her to the picture show the following Saturday. When he reached for her hand, she realized what a pleasant sensation that was. She had not felt this protected since she was a little girl on Papa's knee. Over the next few weeks, she grew fonder of Elbert. He always had exciting plans—like picnics by the lake, a tour of the Piggly Wiggly to show her his work routine, and a Sunday drive.

They fit together nicely and got along well. Both were even-tempered, not easily ruffled. Martha always enjoyed Elbert's company. They studied together, and he was as intelligent and serious about education as she was. Things had settled into a routine.

"You and Elbert are seeing a lot of each other, Martha," Manda had said. "Is it getting serious? Are you in love? Since you are staying with me, I feel responsible for looking out for you, even though I'm not as old as your parents."

"I really like Elbert. Don't see any faults, although I'm sure he has some."

"Do you love him?" She asked again.

"I'm not sure how to tell." Martha had a frown on her face. "Mama says when she first saw Papa, she knew he was the one. Are you supposed to feel sparks or hear bells going off?"

"It wasn't that way with Dick and me. We were friends at first and gradually came to realize we loved each other. We knew a lot about each other before we got serious."

"I think it's that way for me, too. I like him, and that has grown, so maybe at this point I'd say it was love. I trust him; I enjoy being with him. He makes me laugh. I can see a good future with him."

"That may be better than seeing stars and having bells go off," Manda said.

That evening in bed, Martha's mind could not stop thinking about the conversation with Manda. She knew Elbert was getting more serious about their relationship. But how did she really feel about a future with him? He said he wanted to be a merchant, but he was the oldest son and had spent all his life on a farm. Was he expected to take it over? His younger brother Frederick seemed to enjoy farming well enough, but what were his goals? And if she didn't love Elbert enough to be his wife regardless of how he earned a living, was she really in love with him? It was unlike her to be so indecisive. She needed more time.

It went pretty well the first time she took him to meet her family. Mama was cool but cordial, and Martha knew the underlying reason had to do with the preacher match gone wrong. Elbert and Papa got along exceptionally well, which was all the confirmation Martha needed that Elbert was of good character.

Toward the end of the semester, Martha told Elbert she had to go home for the weekend.

"Is everything okay? You seem stressed."

"Everything is okay. Papa needs help with the books at the store, getting ready for tax time."

"But finals are coming up. I thought you said you planned to study all weekend."

"Yes, but Papa needs me."

"Can't it wait? The semester will be over soon."

"No, if he says he needs me, it must be important."

"I'm just thinking about you, Martha. You have needs too."

She thanked him, but there was nothing to be done about it. It was the first time she ever remembered anyone coming to her defense. It was a unique thought to put her needs above those of others. One more "plus" in her deliberations about Elbert.

Chapter 12

MARTHA AND MARRIAGE

They had been skirting around the topic of marriage for some time. He asked, "How many children do you want, Martha?"

"Two," she had answered. "What about you?"

"Two sounds about right. And I hope it's a boy and a girl."

Their romance had advanced, but he was always a gentleman. When he did propose, it was down by the lake after a nice picnic lunch he had fixed. He said he got a discount from the grocery store where he worked. He produced a lovely ring with a small diamond. She had been prepared for his proposal and decided to accept. She loved him and could see them having a good life together.

"Let's get married at the end of the school year. And I have a surprise for you. I want to drive to the place I have my eye on for the store. It has an attached apartment, ideal for us to live in."

Martha liked the location and commented that it was in a good spot for trade. It was in a white neighborhood but on the edge of where the black people had a settlement. "We can serve all the people," she remarked.

Martha and Elbert were married as soon as their second year of college was finished. Neither had planned to go on to a university. Ironically, Reverend Josh officiated the ceremony in the parlor of the Dalton's home, and Mama played the bridal march on the family organ. Elbert's family consisted of only his parents and brother Frederick, but the Dalton clan was stair-stepped girls, all in pretty pastel dresses. John was the proud papa giving Martha away. Abigail was elated to catch the bridal bouquet, and her sisters teased her to no end. Everyone mingled during the reception and enjoyed cake and punch. Martha grinned as she saw Rachel chumming it up with Frederick.

After the reception, Martha and Elbert left for Atlanta in his car, decorated as "Just Married" by his brother Frederick and her brother James. Elbert had worked overtime to earn enough money for a first-class honeymoon for his bride. After their week in the big city, Elbert planned to go to the bank for a loan to buy the store property he had his heart set on. They were both excited about starting something new.

They strolled around the Atlanta streets on their first day, looking in all the big department stores. Martha felt so cosmopolitan. This was her world. On the second day, they went to the zoo and Cyclorama, the exhibit of the Battle of Atlanta during the Civil War. The city had so many entertainment opportunities.

On the third day, when they returned to the hotel from Piedmont Park, the front desk told Elbert he had had a call while he was out with an urgent message to call home. Elbert and Martha both gasped.

His father, who had seemed hale and hearty, had suffered a debilitating stroke, and they were not sure he would survive. So Elbert and Martha quickly packed up and headed south. They were both quiet on the ride home, but they each knew the other was thinking about what this meant to their future plans.

"I don't know what will happen if—."

"Let's not talk about that now, Martha. Let's just pray that everything will be okay." They both resumed their silence.

The news was worse than they thought, and Elbert's father was not expected to make it through the night. He and Martha sat in the hospital waiting room. Frederick had taken his mother home to get a few things. She planned to spend the night.

Elbert told Martha, "I never thought this would happen to Dad." She nodded. She could see the agony on his face.

"I know the crops will need harvesting soon. It will take two healthy men, Elbert." Martha stated what she knew he must realize.

"But... the store...."

"That might have to wait. Frederick can't do it alone."

"Maybe I can find some hired help." She could tell he was conflicted.

"We both know how hard it is to find help. The men who don't have their own farms work either at the sawmill or at the factory."

"He put his head in his hands and bent over. Martha put her arm around him. "I don't see we have any choice right now. The store can wait; the crops can't. You and Frederick can get it done. Then we can look at other options."

"I know you are right. It's just so hard to give up our dream."

"We aren't giving it up."

By the time the crops were in, Elbert and Martha both realized that his grieving mother, Miss Lucille, was in poor health, and they knew it would be best if they stayed there on the farm. There was plenty of room in the big house. Elbert had had to spend his savings on tractor repair, and it seemed in his best interest to plant another crop to recoup his investment. He and Martha talked about trying to run the store in town and run the farm, but the property they wanted had been sold by then.

Chapter 13

MARTHA BACK ON A FARM

Martha was not content with married life. She was still on the farm, albeit a different one. Elbert was not really a farmer, but he had no choice when his father passed away. When Elbert and Martha's daughter was born, Elbert's mother had weathered the mourning period and had found a new interest in her grandbaby.

Their daughter had blond hair like her daddy and was a happy baby, easy to get to sleep. Past the toddler stage, Mattie grew to be an obedient child, and she had plenty of room to play outdoors. She followed her daddy around, talking constantly. When he plowed, his little girl walked behind him in the field. All Elbert had to do was say, "Uh huh," occasionally, and she was content to keep up the chatter.

Martha watched them out of the window and smiled. But she was bored, thinking there had to be more to life than this. Mattie would start school in a few years, and she longed to be off the farm. True, there was plenty of work to keep her busy, but with Miss Lucille being the matriarch of the household and the maid Flossie coming to clean and help with the seasonal chores like canning and making jelly, Martha had a lot of time on her hands.

She and Elbert had considered having another child but now wasn't the time. Whenever she and Elbert talked about it, he said, "I can't believe your mama is still having babies, Martha. Andrew is hardly two years old, and now he has a baby brother. And naming him Henry Lee because Miss Betts says it sounds like a proper preacher's name! She's planning his whole life out for him. Since he's your brother, our little Mattie is older than her uncle!"

Martha nodded. "Mama always said they would have as many children as God sent them. I hope this is the last one. I'm glad you and I have a different idea."

They both thought two children would be a big enough family. She and Elbert agreed on so many things, including that the farm was not their long-term future.

Chapter 14

JAMES AND SALLY ANN

He saw the angry bruise on her leg just before she pulled her skirt down to cover it. Their eyes met. She responded with a shy smile to his concerned, questioning look. She was such a fragile thing; her bones reminded him of a tiny bird. As people say, "skin and bones." But her hair was lovely, a chestnut brown. Her delicate face and twinkly brown eyes promised fun beneath her quiet nature.

She was more than he could ever hope for. He knew he was not handsome—sturdy, solid, big hands, ruddy complexion. By contrast, her skin looked like the cream in the milking jug when it settled on the top.

The teacher's voice drew him back to the lesson. This was his last year of school. He had to try harder to pay attention. Papa said he needed to get as much schooling as possible, but he didn't see the point. Algebra was no good when you were picking cotton.

And he wouldn't be quoting Shakespeare when he was butchering hogs.

When school was finally out, and he was picking up his lunch pail and books, he saw his chance to get near her and pretended he just happened to turn up beside her. She looked up, surprised but pleased.

"You walking my way?" he asked.

"I guess I am if you are going on the Underwood Road." The country roads were known by the most prominent family who lived on them.

With little finesse, he said, "What happened to your leg?" when they were out of earshot of the others.

She wouldn't look him in the eye. "I fell against the rake in the barn. My brother, Johnny, always leaves things where they don't belong."

He kept quiet. *You don't get a bruise that high up on your leg from a rake.*

"Here, let me take your books," he said.

She flinched when he reached toward her. Then she laughed and started pointing out the types of wildflowers. He knew where she lived, a tenant farmer shack behind the Underwood plantation. Before getting too close, she reached for her books, thanked him, and bid him goodbye.

Clearly, she didn't want him coming any closer to her house. He wondered if there was someone there she didn't want him to see. Or maybe there was someone at her house she didn't want to see him.

He waited a few minutes to watch her when she turned off the road. She glanced back and waved, then disappeared among the trees that shaded the house. As he walked on, he thought he heard someone yelling—a man's voice, which sounded angry.

Chapter 15

SALLY ANN AND HER MAMA'S ADVICE

Sally Ann scooted into the house as fast as she could, but not before her father grabbed her arm and, in his drunken slur, said, "Where do you think you're goin', Missy, in such an all-fired hurry? Dontcha have a kiss fer yor' ole man?" His foul breath and rotten-toothed grin made her sick to her stomach.

"Daddy, you know I have to go in and help Mama," she said as she pulled away.

"Mama don't need no help. You little whore, I know what you been up to. I seen that boy with you on the road. You been dartin' into them woods on your way home? I'll show you what happens to little whores like you. You ain't too big for me to take my belt to you!" She backed up, trying to get out of his reach.

Just then, her mother came out onto the porch with a big glass of iced tea. "Here, Herbert, drink this tea, sit down, and rest your gamey leg. I need Sally Ann in the kitchen. I'm making you something special for supper tonight."

"I'm coming, Ma," Sally Ann said as she opened the screen door.

"I'm goin' to the barn," he grumbled. Gertrude and Sally Ann knew he would put some corn liquor in that iced tea.

"Good riddance," she heard Ma whisper, and as he staggered across the yard, she said under her breath, "Maybe he'll pass out, and we won't have to see no more of him tonight. Lord, Lord," Ma shook her head and started back to the kitchen.

"You got homework, honey?"

"A little bit." Sally Ann hugged Ma and put her head on her shoulder.

"Well, you go on and get your lessons, and when you finish, you can come help me. I'm just shucking corn right now." The kitchen was small, hardly big enough for two people.

Sally Ann shared a bedroom with her little sister Bethany; her brother, Johnny, was across the hall. The house was tiny, and the twin beds could barely fit in the room. She didn't have a desk, so she had to sit on her bed with her books spread around her. The dreaded history final exam was only two days away, and she couldn't seem to keep those dates in her head. The worksheet the teacher had given them took all her concentration.

After the history lesson, Sally Ann returned to the kitchen. She sat down at the table with the bowl of beans Ma had picked that morning and started stringing them. They didn't have meat very often, but the garden provided many fresh vegetables. She hated that her mother had to work so hard to keep this family fed. Her daddy had been injured on the combine two years ago and claimed he couldn't work. Mr. Underwood had let them stay at the farm because Johnny was such a good worker, and Ma could work as hard as any man. Johnny had to drop out of school to take over his daddy's job, but that was fine with him.

Sally Ann looked up from snapping beans to see a serious look on Ma's face. "Honey, I want to talk to you about something important. You are in tenth grade now and only have one more year of school. So you need to be thinking about your future."

"I'll get a job, maybe one in town, so I can help out here." Sally Ann had a pervading sense of guilt for not being able to help keep the family going.

"No, that's no kind of life. I was hoping you'd meet some nice boy, and he would take you away from this place. Give you a better life. Maybe someday, take Bethany and me with you. Johnny won't stay here forever, and your daddy can't last long drinking like he does. You a nice-looking girl, and you got to use what you got to attract a man, but make sure he don't love liquor." Sally Ann listened intently.

"You a shy girl, and you got to get over that if you ever gonna catch a man. You got to give 'em what they want, make 'em think they can't live without you. They like a little touchy-feely."

"Ma, I'm shocked you would say that." Sally Ann had never even been kissed.

"And you got to let 'em know you can cook real good and know how to keep house. Treat 'em like they'd be the king of their castle." Ma laughed.

Sally Ann listened intently as Ma continued. "My sister over in Tennessee got her a real good husband from a nice family. She met him in school, and they got lovey-dovey. She turned up pregnant, and her daddy got his shotgun and took her over to his folks' house, and that was that. They got married the next weekend, and now they have a passel of kids and are happy as the day is long. Yes, she did it just right."

Sally Ann didn't say a word. That didn't seem right. She didn't want to trick James, but neither did she want to let him go.

Chapter 16

JAMES TAKES SALLY ANN ON A PICNIC

He could tell she was as excited as he was to go on a picnic. He had invited Sally Ann to see the waterfalls he had created by piling up rocks at the creek. It was deep in the woods on the Dalton place, and except for Louis, nobody ever ventured there. So he hadn't minded the walk to her house on a warm Sunday afternoon. She was waiting out by the road. Her Mama had offered to fix a picnic supper for them.

"Yum, something sure smells good," he said as he took the basket from her. They laughed and talked on the way back to the Dalton place. He had picked up a blanket from the barn and left it out by the fence to get when they walked back to the woods. Nobody in the family had seen him leave. Nobody paid much attention to him anyway, except when there was work to be done.

The woods were quiet except for the noise of their footsteps as they ruffled the fallen leaves and stepped on twigs and the occasional pine cone. There was a slight breeze, and it became darker as they walked farther back, where the trees were thickest.

"Almost there," he said to reassure her.

"What an enchanting place," she said. "And you moved all those rocks? I love the tinkling sound the water makes."

"And I planned the weather just for you," he said as he spread the blanket and indicated she should sit. He told her a funny story about fishing in the creek, where he got too close to the muddy edge and slid in. When she laughed, he said, "I love your laugh, and I love to make you laugh. You deserve to be happy and laugh a lot." He moved closer. He looked at her, but she looked away.

He stretched out and put his hands behind his head. "Aw, I could fall asleep in this peaceful place."

"Why don't you? You deserve a Sunday afternoon nap."

"Only if you will join me." He wanted her to relax too. She always seemed so tense. "Well, come on. Lay back." When she hesitated, he said, "Don't you trust me?"

With that, she lay back and breathed deeply. James closed his eyes and soon felt sleepy.

This was nice, lying beside her.

He woke with a start and blinked, remembering where he was. He looked over at Sally Ann. She was asleep with her mouth slightly open like a rosebud. He smiled and moved closer. He kissed her on the cheek, and she slowly opened her eyes and smiled. "James Dalton, you stole a kiss," she said.

"Yes, and I feel like robbing the whole bank," he said. Sally Ann didn't move and still looked dreamy and sleepy. When he hovered over her face, she looked up. He saw eagerness in her eyes as he leaned forward and kissed her on the lips. She didn't resist but didn't respond.

"Is that okay?" he asked. Sally Ann nodded. He put his hand on her face and ran his fingers through her hair. "You are so lovely." His hand moved down to the opening in her blouse. She gasped, but he left his hand there, and she relaxed. She raised her hand and touched his face. It felt so good to have another human being touch him. He had not realized how much he craved affection.

He kissed her again, and this time, she did respond. He felt like a fire had been set in him. Without conscious intent, his hand found her leg and moved upward. She grew stiff.

"James, we can't! What if something happens; what if I get... you know?"

He looked her square in the eyes.

"Let it happen. I love you and want you with me always."

He kissed her neck and her ear. She closed her eyes and let out a big sigh. He could feel her body relax as she moved closer to him.

Anybody who grew up on a farm knows what happens next, he thought. It's built into nature. It was going to be a good summer.

Chapter 17

JAMES TELLS PAPA HIS NEWS

The air was chilly as James took a deep breath and walked into the barn. He knew Papa would be putting fresh hay into the stalls. Without saying a word, he picked up another pitchfork and silently began to help his father. James opened his mouth several times and started to say something but stopped short. He could feel Papa's patience wearing thin, so finally he blurted out, "Papa, there's a girl I like."

He was relieved to see Papa's smile and was comforted by his words. "Well, good, son. That's the way God intended it."

If it had been Mama or any of his sisters, they'd have pounded him with all kinds of questions right away. But James always felt more at ease with Papa, knowing he would let him take his time. Even so, he dreaded what his father would say, so he spoke first, trying to put *him* at ease.

"It's Sally Ann Johnson from down the road." He didn't dare look up at Papa, but he did notice out of the corner of his eye that Papa stopped for just a second before resuming his task of pitching hay.

Then he heard the judgment in Papa's voice. "That tenant family that lives on the Underwood Place?" James only nodded, and Papa continued.

"Better be careful, son. I hear ol' man Johnson stays drunk most of the time and gets meaner the more he drinks. The moonshiners keep him supplied."

James quickly replied, "I haven't seen it, but I think he knocks Sally Ann around. She won't say, but I've seen bruises on her."

He saw Papa wince as he said, "Drink makes some men mean." James thought about how different Papa acted when he went on one of his infrequent binges. When that happened, Papa just wanted to be left alone to sleep. Yes, the Johnson family was different.

Then, as if to reassure himself, James added, "I think I love her."

He saw the concern on Papa's face and heard the sincerity in his voice. "Don't confuse love with feeling sorry for someone, son. It's only natural that good men like you want to rescue a damsel in distress. The best thing we can do is pray for them and let God handle this situation."

The silence was poignant. In a moment, Papa continued as if to convince James. "You are just finishing high school. You've got a lot of years before you get serious and look for a wife. Then I'll give you some property, and you can build a fine house for you and your family right here on the Dalton land. God will send you the right one when it's time."

James knew his father's advice was sound, but he didn't want to hear it. He stammered, "Well, the thing is, I think it's time." He hung his head and refused to look at Papa, who had stopped with the fork in mid-air.

He could sense Papa staring at him for a long time and knew he was putting together the pieces that would reveal the whole picture.

"Boy, you are in a lot of trouble. This will kill your mama."

"I know, but what can I do?"

"Does her daddy know? If he does, he'll be coming up here with a shotgun."

"I don't think so. She's only about three months along, but she won't be able to hide it much longer. She only told me last week." He knew what Papa would say. He was right.

Papa took a deep breath and looked off through the open barn door in the distance. "There's only one thing to do. You must do right by her and have a wedding as soon as possible. And you have to be a man and tell your Mama. I'll go with you to help her through this."

James knew he had to swallow his medicine, and after supper, he and Papa took Mama into the bedroom and closed the door. That dreaded conversation turned out to be worse than he had expected. He told her the unwelcome news and had to stand there while she scolded him.

"My firstborn son! You've disgraced me. You've disgraced all your sisters. Brought shame to our family name. And to think I named you for my grandfather because I wanted you to be a preacher like him. Now it's all over. I'll never be able to hold my head up again. I can't go to church anymore. Everyone will be talking about us!"

He thought it would never end, Mama wailing as he felt nothing but shame and guilt. All he could say was "Yes, ma'am," as she berated and wailed at him.

"If I had known you were interested in that girl, I'd have told you what a sorry family she comes from. I could have told you she'd try to trap you. She just wants to escape that bad home she's from. I won't accept her into this family—never. You certainly can't bring her into this house to be such a bad example to your sisters and to be under my nose all day."

When he finally left, he saw his sisters, Lydia and Abigail, washing and drying the supper dishes at the sink. When they raised their eyebrows at him, he knew they were wondering what he had done that had caused such a ruckus. Well, let them wonder.

A week later, Lydia told James that Papa had made a startling announcement at the Sunday dinner table. Papa shared how James and Sally Ann had eloped three months ago but had just now decided to announce it. The couple was told they would make a home in the old quarters kept for the hired help across the road at the far end of the family property. James would continue to help Papa with the farm and timber but would now be paid like any other hired help.

"Oh, good, a wedding celebration!" Phoebe had glowed.

"Harrumph," Mama had reportedly said, "All the celebrating is over."

Chapter 18

SALLY ANN BECOMES MRS. DALTON

Sally Ann was overjoyed to be Mrs. James Dalton. They had worked together to clean the cobwebs and animal droppings in their new living quarters. It had been originally built to accommodate the hired help in the late 1870s. The cabin had two rooms. The front room served as the living, dining, and kitchen, while the other was a small bedroom. There was no indoor plumbing but an outhouse behind.

A nice feature of the house was a spacious front porch. The first night they sat on the steps, James complained about the loud noise the cicadas made, but Sally Ann said it sounded like peaceful music to her ears. In addition, she loved the big oak tree that provided shade.

Despite their living accommodations, Sally Ann knew James was happy to be married and that he loved her. She tried to be everything he ever wanted in a wife, and she didn't complain, no matter what.

She knew James resented how his parents treated him, but she knew he had disappointed them with a shotgun wedding. She could see he had decided to accept his lot in life. He struggled to keep up with his work, so she tried to make his life comfortable when he came home every day.

There was a knock on the door. Sally Ann was surprised to see Martha and cordially invited her in. She was trying hard to make this small cabin into a home with old cast-out furniture. She was embarrassed for Martha to see things like this and imagined her sister-in-law thinking, "Poor James."

Instead, Martha greeted her warmly and asked if there was anything she could do to help them get established. Sally Ann was at a loss for words at this kind gesture, and tears appeared in her eyes.

"I'm sorry for the problems I've caused."

Martha moved to put her arms around Sally Ann and said, "I've never seen James smile so much. He's happy, and I hope you are too."

"Yes, I love him and want to be the best wife ever."

She recognized that Martha, always sensible, got right to the point. "I came here to welcome you to the family. It's a big one, and there are lots of different opinions. Some of us will take longer than others to get used to the idea. But we are Christian people, and everyone will come around, eventually. My advice is to just be who you are, and when others accept how happy you are making James, they will love you too."

Sally Ann felt genuine relief and appreciation, which showed on her face. Martha said goodbye, explaining that she had chores waiting for her back at the house.

Chapter 19

JAMES CUTS TIMBER

Louis Jacobs rode up on a horse from the barn to join the men in the Dalton woods. He had come to help James and his daddy on timber-cutting day. The three men would work all day until they had a wagonload of logs to take to the sawmill.

"Mornin' Mr. John. James."

"Morning, Louis," replied Mr. Dalton. James only nodded.

Louis was a little shy around Mr. Dalton and stayed quiet until spoken to.

"Now that you have finished school, Louis, what do you plan to do?" Mr. Dalton quizzed.

"I'm hoping to get on at the sawmill."

"Your family all doing okay?" Mr. Dalton continued.

"Yes, sir. Mama has been a little poorly, but she's better now."

"How about your sisters?"

"Mean as ever," Louis said with a grin and a chuckle, then added, "Nah, they all right."

After a brief bit of chitchat, Mr. Dalton explained the work plan for the day, and the three of them got busy. It would be a long day.

James cut the tree in the way they wanted it to fall. The two of them then got the cross saw and went to work, back and forth and back and forth. They straightened up and rubbed their backs when the tree finally fell. Mr. Dalton took over limbing the tree.

Next, they put the chain around the log and had the horse drag it closer to the wagon. Then, while they went to work on the next tree, Mr. Dalton marked the log every six feet where it would be cut into the size preferred by the sawmill.

All three men would then pick up a log and stack it on the wagon. They worked as a team until noon when they stopped for lunch. They each found a tree to lean against, ate the lunches, and drank the tea the womenfolk had sent.

At the end of the day, with the wagon loaded with logs, James and Louis headed to the lumberyard while Mr. Dalton rode Louis' horse back to the barn. The ride was pleasant, a reprieve before they had to unload the logs. They drove into the lumberyard next to the railroad tracks. The mill pond was full of logs, and they saw a fellow worker walking on the logs, separating them into sizes and grades.

The yard superintendent met them at the entrance of the sawmill and measured the stack of logs. They would be paid according to this measurement, so James got off the wagon to make sure the correct numbers were recorded. He was handed a piece of paper which he would take to the cashier as soon as the logs were unloaded. They drove further into the log pile to start unloading.

"How ya doing, James? You got a big load today. You boys going to be able to unload by yourselves?"

"I reckon so, seeing as we loaded by ourselves." James was offended that their ability was questioned. These old geezers always acted like they were so smart.

When all was unloaded, James started for the cashier window. Louis followed as he was eager to see how much their work had amounted to in case he ever had his own land.

James said, "You go on back to the wagon, Louis."

Louis looked taken aback but stopped and headed in the other direction. Just as he reached the wagon, he turned around in time to see James pull some bills out of the big wad of cash and stuff them into his pants pocket. When he joined Louis in the wagon, James put the remaining wad of bills in his pants pocket and said, "We did right good today. Papa should pay you and me some good wages for all this work."

Chapter 20

LYDIA PROVOKES MAMA

At the next Sunday dinner, Lydia suddenly said, "I miss James. Why aren't he and Sally Ann here?" She registered Mama's stern look that meant, "Keep quiet." Lydia knew Mama would not want to say why they weren't invited in front of the little ones at the table.

Lydia continued as if she were ignorant of that, "I really like Sally Ann. She is very sweet and very appreciative of their new living quarters. She has fixed it up to be very cozy, and I've never seen James so happy."

Mama didn't answer, and Lydia noted that Papa kept quiet with his eyes firmly locked on the food on his plate. Finally, Abigail spoke up, "I can go down and invite them to Sunday supper this evening. It will be fun to get to know her."

Lydia expected Mama's remark, "There will be no supper tonight. Since we had a big dinner, we will just have a glass of buttermilk and cornbread. There will be no invitation."

Abigail continued, clueless. "Well, they probably would love that. It's not the food but the thought that counts, right, Mama?"

"If you are so determined to visit with them, you can go down there, Abigail, and that goes for the rest of you, too!" Mama exclaimed. Lydia looked innocently at Mama, whose expression made it clear that her word was final and the subject was closed.

Lydia was reading in her favorite living room chair when she heard Martha and Elbert drive up for their usual Sunday afternoon visit. She looked out the window to see them get out of the car. Lydia saw Abigail run out to meet them and noticed how she was talking animatedly to Martha, no doubt about the dinnertime conversation.

The couple stayed for the buttermilk and cornbread supper. Papa and Elbert walked to the barn, and Lydia watched Martha steer Mama into the bedroom. Then, Lydia went outside to the flower garden that just happened to be below the bedroom window. She could hear the conversation clearly.

"Mama, I heard you didn't want to invite James and Sally Ann for Sunday supper. You know Sally Ann will be the mother of your first grandchild. The first

Dalton of the next generation. Surely that innocent one deserves a loving and welcoming family."

Mama sounded defiant.

"Harrumph. Well, you can't blame me. I disapprove of her behavior and won't act like everything is fine with me."

"What about your son's behavior?" Martha gently asked.

"Nor his either, but it's up to the woman to say 'no.'"

"I guess since Adam and Eve, humans have disappointed God, but it's a good thing we can all be forgiven. If God can forgive, surely we can too."

Lydia didn't hear any more of the conversation, but she could imagine Mama pursing her lips and lifting her head high like she was still Miss Preacher's Daughter.

Chapter 21

LYDIA STARTS NURSING SCHOOL

Since Martha and James had both married and left home, Lydia was now the oldest. She didn't intend to be the family's old maid, stuck at home caring for Mama and Papa in their old age. Lydia wanted adventure and had to be daring to ever get that life. She had to figure out how to escape her circumstances and get into something better.

Mama had agreed to her starting nursing school in town at the local hospital. Maybe she would meet some rich doctor, which would be her ticket. Then, at least, she would escape the farm. Lydia would begin in the fall and was eager to get started.

Papa had driven Lydia to the school with just a few belongings, as the admission letter had instructed.

He had been full of advice throughout the journey. As if she wouldn't know these things already.

"You know you are being given a great opportunity, so you want to make the most of it. Remember, your reputation affects the whole family. Study hard, follow the rules, and you will do just fine. It will be nice to have a nurse in the family. Mama is bursting with pride, and you'll be a good example for your sisters."

And I'm escaping that dreary farm, Lydia thought to herself. She didn't know quite what to expect, but she had visions of the glamorous life that awaited her in the stiff white uniform that would command respect. Of course, she would be on the lookout for a handsome young doctor.

Papa had dropped her off with her suitcase, as men weren't allowed in the dorm. She waved goodbye and entered the stately hall. There was a long corridor, very pristine and deadly quiet. She found a registration desk at the end of the hall and received her room assignment. The registrar told Lydia the class's first meeting was at 6 p.m. in the first-floor classroom. She had two hours to get settled and find her way to the place where she would begin her new life.

Lydia headed up the stairs of the dorm in search of her assigned room with curiosity about who her roommate would be. She hoped it would not be some prim and proper "do-gooder" because she was ready for a bit of freedom and opportunity to explore forbidden fun.

She thought of Mama's admonishment, "Be careful what you wish for."

"Wanna cigarette?" were the first words Lydia heard coming from this creature sitting on the bed by the window as she entered her dormitory room.

"What?" said Lydia, who couldn't believe her eyes! This tomboy-looking girl with extremely short, straight hair, wearing what looked like her daddy's pants and a button-down shirt, sat cross-legged as big as you please, blowing smoke rings. "I thought smoking wasn't allowed in the nurses' quarters," Lydia stammered.

"Well, I'm not a nursing student yet. So what are they going to do, throw me out before I ever get started? Besides, I have the window open so no one can smell the smoke. My name is Lily Jane. What's yours?"

"Lydia," she replied quietly, sensing that Lily Jane was trying to establish her dominance.

"Lily Jane and Lydia. I think we will get along just fine. I hope you don't mind that I chose the bed by the window. It'll come in handy when I feel the need for a smoke."

Lydia was used to sharing with seven sisters, but now as the oldest at home, she had felt entitled to have the first choice. "Oh, sure, the other bed is fine with me." She found herself at a loss for words to protest. A little resentment surfaced as she saw that Lily Jane had chosen the bigger closet, too. She would have to be clever in handling this new relationship.

Lily Jane and Lydia sat near the back of the classroom—the better to survey everyone, Lily Jane had said. There were twelve members of the class, girls from various small towns throughout southern Georgia. First, the teacher introduced herself as Miss Marshall.

"Obviously, an old maid," whispered Lily Jane. Lydia gave her full attention to the speaker, slightly annoyed with Lily Jane's side comments.

"You will be up at 5:30 a.m., take care of your morning hygiene, make your bed, and present yourself at breakfast fully dressed in uniform at 6:15 a.m. The class will begin promptly at 7:00 a.m. in this room. You will have class all day for six weeks while learning basic nursing skills.

"After that, your classes will be in the mornings, and you will report to the wards from noon to 7 p.m. You will have thirty minutes each for lunch and dinner in the hospital dining room. Your study time will be when you return to the dorm that evening. Lights out at 10 p.m."

She went on to elaborate on other rules. Sunday was the day off. Girls could have visitors in the parlor with supervision. Uniforms were never to be worn in public. Miss Marshall finished with a frown. "No males in the dorm halls or rooms—ever!"

The next day, all went according to schedule. Lunch was in the hospital cafeteria, next door to the nurses' dorm. The students had a separate dining room, the better to hear a spontaneous lecture or class announcements. There was much chatter during lunch as the twelve novices sought to learn more about each other.

Carol was plump and jovial but didn't appear too bright. Loretta had been nodding off during the morning class; *what was her problem?* June seemed bright and lively, maybe a little egotistical and competitive. Betty was beautiful but had a sullen expression and seemed a little paranoid. Angie looked like she belonged in the movies, not in a nurse's uniform. Was she really serious about this austere life?

Anne was fun-loving, a little spoiled, and had asked many questions whose answers were obvious to everyone else. Maureen clearly thought she would be the teacher's pet; she raised her hand quickly to show she knew the answer. Nancy was quiet as a mouse, content to watch and listen. Joy seemed bright and with a good sense of humor. Sue Ann looked sickly and scared to death.

With the group, Lily Jane was the show-off character, the daredevil. She didn't seem intimidated by the authority figures at the school. Lydia was determined to be quiet and not draw attention to herself. She wanted to succeed.

Before the afternoon class, the students were measured for uniforms: a blue dress hemmed to mid-calf, a detachable white collar and cuffs, and a white apron. They were also to wear nude-colored hose (white once they graduated) and sturdy white shoes, and after a successful three months, they earned a white cap.

Students had to have a watch with a sweeping second hand to count pulse and respirations. Martha had given her a watch as a gift and emphasized the family's confidence in her and their expectations. It was the first watch Lydia had ever owned.

The school would furnish a pair of scissors for each student to be used for cutting tape or for other medical needs. They would keep the scissors tucked between the two buttons in the waistband of their aprons. The uniforms would arrive after the six weeks of basic training in the classroom. The hospital would provide laundry services.

What Miss Marshall didn't say, but what was to become evident to the class, was that in exchange for this education, the students were a significant source of labor for the hospital, getting more proficient as their studies progressed. By the third and final year, they would be practically running the hospital.

The first week was exhausting, but the girls had settled into a routine. Work, eat, study, sleep. Then, wake up and do it all over again.

"You have a fella?" Lily Jane asked out of the blue.

"What? No, I don't. But I will be looking once we get in the hospital."

"Well, mine is coming to see me tomorrow night."

Lydia was confused. "But we can only have visitors on Sunday," Lydia reminded Lily Jane.

"I don't intend to see him in the parlor with that nosy housemother, Miss Rozelle, spying on us. I'll meet him underneath the pecan tree in the back of the dorm after it's dark."

"But what if you are caught? You'd be sent home immediately. What would your parents say?"

"Oh, I don't plan to get caught. I'll leave a rock in the back door to keep it slightly open, and I'll sneak back in after curfew when everyone is in bed."

"You are a daredevil, all right," Lydia said with clear admiration.

Lydia woke to the sound of a soft ping. It was coming from the window. She listened and heard it again.

Then she heard someone say her name. She was careful not to look out the window, but she quickly surmised it was Lily Jane who needed her to come open the door to the building.

Well, she had warned Lily Jane that she could get caught. Someone had probably removed the rock doorstop and the door automatically locked. *Too bad for her*, Lydia thought. She wasn't about to get in trouble aiding Lily Jane in her foolish scheme. Let her suffer the consequences.

She heard voices coming from outside. It sounded like Miss Rozelle, and her voice was raised. About ten minutes later, Lydia heard a whisper in the hall, "And be quiet not to wake the other girls who follow the rules and are in bed where they are supposed to be." She heard their dorm room door open and sensed Lily Jane tiptoeing in. Lydia kept very still and quiet. She heard rustling like Lily Jane undressing, and then she heard the creak of the mattress springs. She smiled to herself. Girls who did foolish things had to pay the price.

The next morning Lydia feigned innocence as Lily Jane recounted what had happened. Sure enough, she returned to the dorm at about 2 a.m. and found the door was no longer propped open.

"I tried to signal you to come open the door, Lydia."

"Oh, you know what a deep sleeper I am."

"Old Battleaxe heard the noise and came to investigate. I 'bout died when the door opened, and instead of your face, I saw hers! She made me come into her room and gave me a dressing down. Said she'd decide my punishment tomorrow. I don't care. I had a good time with my honey, and it was worth it. You don't know what you're missing—too bad you slept through the whole adventure!"

Lydia chuckled quietly to herself.

Chapter 22

LYDIA HAS A GENTLEMAN CALLER

The nurse's cap transformed her into a different person. She was disappointed she had not met any eligible doctor yet. The first three months had been hard, but she had made it. She could now take vital signs (blood pressure, temperature and pulse), change linens with a person in the bed, safely transfer a patient from bed to stretcher, and many other skills. Lydia admired herself in the crisp uniform. The work was okay, but it was exhausting. It wasn't as physically taxing as farm work, but it was just as constant.

On Sunday afternoon, she and Lily Jane were studying in their room when there was a knock on the door. A student assistant to the housemother entered and said, "You have a visitor downstairs—a gentleman."

"Who does?" Lydia and Lily Jane both said at once. Lily Jane was on restrictions with no visitors for a month.

"For Lydia," the student assistant replied.

Lily Jane looked surprised and said, "Lydia?" at the same time Lydia said, "Me?"

"Well, it must be my brother, James. There must be something wrong at home." Lydia didn't bother to check herself in the mirror like Lily Jane always did when a visitor for her was announced. Instead, she entered the parlor and looked around for James but gasped when she saw Walter waiting with his hat in hand.

"Walter, what are you doing here?"

"Why, I've come to see you. I recently stopped at your Papa's store and learned you were in this nursing school. So I decided to come by on my next trip to Atlanta to see you."

At the exact moment that she remembered her manners, Lydia also recalled that she had not checked her hair and probably looked a mess! Nevertheless, she decided to make the best of it and invited Walter to sit down with her on one of the settees on the east side of the room to avoid the sun. Then, just as she had learned to make conversation with patients and their families, she began to ask Walter to tell her about his recent trips to Atlanta and asked how the weather in Florida was.

After some polite chitchat, Walter asked if she would be able to go for a short ride in the countryside. This was a welcome idea to Lydia, who, even though she didn't particularly like the farm, had missed seeing that scenery. She signed out at the front desk, and they proceeded to Walter's car. He pointed out he had a new one since he had last taken her for a ride. This one looked even more luxurious, and she got that exhilarated feeling of adventure again.

After driving for a while, Walter asked if she would like to stop for a coke. It had been too long since she had enjoyed anything but hospital cafeteria food, so she readily agreed. When he stopped the car, Walter reached over and took her hand instead of getting out.

"Lydia, I hope you don't mind me calling on you. I realized how much I had looked forward to seeing you on my trips. And my heart sank when I learned you were no longer at the store. I hope you don't think the difference in our ages is a problem. I'm forty, but I feel like a twenty-year-old when I'm with you. I have strong feelings for you and want to call on you again."

Lydia could not say that she was shocked. She had sensed all along that Walter was interested. When she turned on the charm, Lydia saw him wrapped around her finger. She batted her eyes and smiled, "That would be nice. I would like that too."

She expected the teasing by Lily Jane when she returned to her room, but she was unprepared for the criticism.

"He's too old for you! He wouldn't be any fun. He'd want to sit by the fire and read a book instead of going out dancing."

"Well, maybe I would prefer reading, too," Lydia replied, a little crushed with Lily Jane's disapproval. "At least he is mature and comes to the front door instead of the fire exit door!"

Lily Jane ignored the barb. "I'm going to fix you up with one of Al's friends and show you what real fun is. In case you get serious about this Walter guy, at least you will have known what you missed out on."

Lydia cut off the conversation with, "We'd better get back to studying. Test tomorrow."

Chapter 23

LYDIA AND JAMES

L ydia had the weekend off and decided to spend it on the farm with the family. Everyone was eager to hear her stories, and the younger girls wanted her to listen to their hearts with her new stethoscope. It was nice to eat Mama's cooking for a change. And she enjoyed being treated like a guest instead of having to do farm chores. After supper Saturday night, Lydia announced she was going to walk over to James' house for a visit. She saw Mama stiffen.

"James, tell me what's going on with Mama. Has she gotten over her snit about you marrying Sally Ann?"

"She says she will never get over it, that I disgraced her."

"Well, we both know how stubborn she is. And rigid. Once she takes a position, she thinks it's a sign of weak character to change her mind."

"She quotes scripture about sin, but she never quotes those about forgiveness."

"I know lots of people, even some in our Beulah community, whose first baby came a little too early. But most of them go on about life."

"Mama thinks because she was a preacher's daughter, she sits up on some pedestal. She really thought I might become a preacher." James shook his head and smirked at the idea.

"And what about Papa? How does he treat you?"

"He never mentions Sally Ann or asks me how she is doing. I think Mama has given him strict orders to shun her. He gave us this shitty place to live in and pays me the same as Louis."

"But you are the oldest son! Who else is going to care about this big farm? You are sure to get it one day."

"I don't know. Mama would die before she would let Sally Ann and me move into the big house."

"Well, have you thought about moving away? Working full time at the sawmill? Working someone else's farm?"

"I love this place, have always loved it. It's my home. I always dreamed someday it would be mine. I deserve it. You know how hard I've worked all these years."

"Yes, I do know. But how can you stand to be treated like this?"

"I'm just biding my time. I can do without Mama if she wants to be so coldhearted. I can be coldhearted, too. Sally Ann is all I need. I'll keep my little family down here, and we will be just fine."

They were silent for a moment as they each thought about how life had turned out. Just then, Sally Ann came out on the porch to join them.

James slapped his knees. "Tell me about you, Lydia. How is school? Had any adventures?"

"School is okay. Lots of studying. The work is hard, and they give us first-year students all the sickest patients."

"Do you ever get to have any fun?" asked Sally Ann.

"Walter came by to see me and took me for a ride. That was nice. And my roommate, Lily Jane, is going to fix me up with a blind date. She's a bit of a rebel, so no telling what I am in for."

"My advice is to enjoy life, Lydia. Don't hold back," James said.

Chapter 24

LYDIA HAS A BLIND DATE

Lily Jane was faithful to her word and told Lydia that Al and his friend Richard were picking them up next Sunday. Al had a boat, and they would go to the river for the afternoon. Lydia had formed a picture of Al in her mind, although she had never met him. But she was wrong; he wasn't a good-for-nothing redneck but a handsome young man with good manners. He and Lily Jane were very comfortable with each other, and she could sense genuine affection.

But if Lydia thought Al was handsome, his friend Richard was a stunner. He had a little of the "bad boy" appearance, but his manners were charming. Lydia felt excited and looked forward to some risqué fun. Al had an old beat-up car; the boat and trailer were hitched to the back.

The two boys sat in the front, the girls in the back. As soon as they were out of sight and on the road, the guys popped the top off a bottle of beer and handed each of the girls one. Lydia had never had a beer before, but she accepted it without knowing what else to do. She was surprised to see Lily Jane take a big swallow.

"Phew!" said Lydia after her first tiny sip, screwing up her face like a prune. "Tastes like rotten eggs."

Lily Jane gave her a disapproving look and said, "Girl, it's 1930. Everybody's doing it. Keep drinking. It will grow on you."

Taking tiny sips, Lydia finally got a half bottle down. Suddenly everything was funny, and she giggled at everything Lily Jane said. The boys were whooping it up with their beers, tossing the empty bottles on the roadside. Lydia felt free like she could do anything she wanted to with no pangs of conscience.

They reached the lake, and while the boys launched the boat, the girls changed into their bathing suits in the car.

"Scooch down, and nobody will see you," Lily Jane instructed.

"Roomie, you have taught me so many bad habits."

The guys had worn their swimming trunks but removed their shirts when they got in the boat. It was fabulous fun to speed around and watch the skiers. Al handled the steering wheel in one hand and a beer in the other. Lily Jane whispered something in Al's ear, and he put the boat in idle. She hopped over the side but held onto the boat.

"What are you doing, Lily Jane?" Lydia asked.

"Well, I don't see a bathroom out here, do you?" Both the girls started giggling again as Lily Jane indicated she needed a hand to get back in the boat.

On the way home, Al asked Richard to drive so he and Lily Jane could sit in the back seat. Lydia heard noises coming from back there but didn't turn around. When Richard told her to slide over to sit next to him, she did. He had wandering hands, but Lydia told him to keep both hands on the wheel. He laughed but didn't try anything else except a wet kiss when they arrived back at the dorm.

That night she wrote all about the escapade in her journal. She had wanted adventures, but really, did she want a life like this? The experience made her feel she could be somebody different, carefree, who liked fun above all else—someone who didn't care about the consequences. But it didn't feel as good as she had thought it would.

The following day, Lydia felt awful. She couldn't concentrate in class, and all she wanted to do at the hospital that afternoon was sit at the nurses' desk. Lydia couldn't help thinking about the contrast between Walter and Richard. With Walter, she felt she was in control of the relationship. A relationship with Richard seemed a little scary. But the call of adventure was there. If he asked her out again, she wouldn't refuse.

Chapter 25

JAMES TAKES SALLY ANN TO CHURCH

James was pleased with the clean-up job in the little cabin that was his new home with Sally Ann. It no longer smelled so musty. It was in reasonably good repair, with no ceiling leaks or gaps in the wood walls. He had cleaned the years of old ashes out of the pot-bellied stove. It was adequate to give them warmth in the winter and serve as a stove to cook on. It would have to do for now.

He vowed he would provide Sally Ann with a better home as soon as possible. He didn't know how or when it would be likely because the nominal wages he got from Papa were barely enough for essentials. He would resurrect the old garden plot out back. Sally Ann would love having something of her own to nurture. Papa had given him one milk cow and Uncle Gene had given him an old iron bed and mattress and a couple of wooden chairs. James could make a kitchen table out of old scrap lumber on the place. The cabin had windows on each side, and he had gone to Mama's sewing basket when she wasn't around and taken some old but colorful feed sacks that would have to do for curtains.

James grew more and more resentful at being treated so shabbily. As the oldest son, he should be treated as the heir apparent, but he had been labeled the family's outcast. The girls seemed to have anything they wanted while he had scraps from the family table. Goodness! He wasn't even invited to the family table. He was treated like a pariah—not fit to sit down with the pious Dalton clan. He tried not to let his bitterness show to Papa. At least Papa was willing to help him in ways Mama wouldn't hear about. He knew it was a strain for Papa to shell out wages for work he had always gotten for free.

Sally Ann, on the other hand, told him she was thrilled with her new home. "How spacious," she had said. James looked at her like she was joking, but he saw she was sincere.

"All this space where I don't have to walk on eggshells in fear of my daddy," Sally Ann had said.

He found her to be ambitious, too. She set to work with a broom and mop and kept the place spic and span. Her mother came over, helped her make the curtains fit, and brought some old rag scraps to make a rug. James was pleased with his new wife.

Sally Ann had changed dresses three times, asking his opinion about what women wore to Beulah Baptist Church. She was as excited as a young girl going to her first prom. When he had first suggested they go to church, he saw the fear in her eyes before it quickly vanished with her desire to please him. He knew she thought this might be an opportunity to heal the breach with his family. And if he were honest, that was a faint hope he harbored, too.

Not wanting to risk rejection, he didn't ask Papa to pick them up in the buggy to ride to church. Instead, after he saw the family pass by, James went to the big house, got the two-seater shay and hitched up Maude.

"Now, be gentle because my wife is six months pregnant, you hear?" He patted her face, and she blinked her tired, old eyes. She would give them a slow ride through the country on this beautiful day.

If the weather was pleasant, the custom was families arrived early and mingled on the hallowed church grounds. Then, when the pastor was ready to begin, someone would clang the church bell on the porch, signaling for everyone to go inside and get seated. James had timed it well. Just as they arrived, the bell was ringing. He helped Sally Ann up the steps and into the vestibule. He knew Mama had seen them, but she looked straight ahead as she took her place on the organ bench. Papa was up front to lead the singing. He saw James and Sally Ann and gave them a broad smile and a nod of approval.

James didn't plan to sit up front on the family pew with his sisters. He knew all church eyes would be watching for any subtle sign of family disharmony. Besides, he wanted his own pew to establish that he was a separate family now, and someday his children would fill the row.

As they entered the church, Mrs. Jordan looked up with a smile that quickly faded, and she turned her back on Sally Ann rather than speak. James clenched his jaw, and his ruddy complexion deepened. Sally Ann didn't seem to notice and looked around in awe at the chandelier and the velvet pew cushions like she was seeing a fairy wonderland. James was headed down the center aisle when an usher blocked his way and motioned to seats in the back row. James stood there frozen, undecided as to whether he should push his way forward, turn and storm out of the church, or quietly turn away wrath and sit on the back row. He decided on the latter.

Sally Ann hadn't known the hymns, but she thoroughly enjoyed them. She whispered to James, "Your parents are so talented. I wish I could play the organ like Miss Betts. And your father has such a booming voice."

James couldn't carry a tune, so he remained silent while the congregation sang. He could tell that Sally Ann was confused about when to stand and when to sit down, but she followed his lead. When the little congregation stood to pledge allegiance to the American flag, she proudly put her hand over her heart and recited along with everyone else. When they all turned and began to pledge allegiance to the Christian flag, she stood silently while everyone else said:

"I pledge Allegiance to the Christian Flag and to the Savior for whose kingdom it stands, one brotherhood uniting all mankind in service and in love."

Damn, he should have taught her that before they came. He noticed eyes on her mute lips. What the hell did he care; they wouldn't be returning, not with the snubbing they had received. So much for uniting all brotherhood in love. He didn't plan to stick around and give them a further opportunity, and during the last hymn, James pulled on Sally Ann's arm, and they quietly exited the church. She smiled at him, but with a puzzled look on her face, she obediently followed him outside.

"Come on, I want us to walk out to the cemetery. I will show you where my grandparents are buried. It's at the back of this lot." He managed to linger over the gravesites of his Dalton relatives long enough to allow the churchgoers to leave him in peace. Then, he saw an older couple headed his way. It was the Millers, whose family plot was next to the Daltons' plot. He had gone to school with their eldest son, B.J.

"Morning, Mr. Miller, Miz Miller," James said politely.

"Why, James, nice to see you, and this must be your lovely bride."

James introduced them and was proud of Sally Ann's manners. Then, he asked, "Is B. J. with you? I haven't seen him in a coon's age."

"No, he took a job at the sawmill over in Pasco County, and they are so busy he has to work on Sundays. Lots of building is going on around these parts. You and your daddy still cutting timber?"

"Yes, sir. Our woods need thinning out, and we've got a-plenty." He paused and got up the courage to ask, "You know if they're hiring on at the sawmill?"

"B.J. says they are. If not full time, then whatever an able-bodied man can spare."

"Well, nice to see y'all, and tell ol' B.J. I said don't be a stranger." James had just solved his problem explaining why he wasn't attending church anymore.

James was up early every morning, including Saturdays, to head up to the big house and help Papa with the day's chores. Of course, it hurt that Mama avoided him, but he didn't say anything to anyone. He'd be damned if he would kowtow to her after all the years he had slaved away on this farm for her to enjoy the good life. Her and his sisters never doing a lick of hard work outside.

"I heard B.J. Miller has got his self a job over at the Pasco County sawmill. I'm thinking about going over there and seeing if they need any extra help on my day off, Sunday," James said.

Papa was silent.

"I could maybe pick up some extra lumber that didn't make the grade for selling and bring it home. I figure it'll take 7500 board feet to build us a three-room house. I want to build Sally Ann and me a house and then use the cabin for a summer kitchen. It makes the house awfully hot to fire up the stove in the summer just to cook."

Papa responded, "We need to do some logging in Grandma's woods, anyway. We got plenty. You can have a tenth of all you cut down."

"Much obliged." James was humiliated that he practically had to beg for lumber to make a decent house when the family woods were bursting with trees. And he would have to cut down nine for the family's profits before he could have a measly one.

It was the first Sunday James had worked at the sawmill, and he was late getting home for supper. Sally Ann did the best she could cooking on the pot-bellied stove, but she was limited to only the one pan, a cast-iron skillet he had taken from Mama's enormous supply.

So tonight, all they had was bacon and fried hoecakes—no way to do any baking. They ate hurriedly because James had to go to the big house to slop the hogs. It was dusk when he reached the back porch and found the slop pail with the day's leftovers—apple peelings, sweet potatoes, cornbread, cucumber peelings, and what looked like sausage gravy. It was packed to the brim. He grabbed it up and stomped to the pig pen.

"If I was blind, I could still find it by the pig shit smell," he said to no one in particular. The greedy, dirty bastards raced to the trough, nosing each other out of the way and grunting like they were starving to death. He threw the slop over the fence, not caring that some of it landed on their heads.

Chapter 26

MARTHA GETS A JOB

That evening, sitting on the porch drinking iced tea with Elbert and little Mattie, Martha broached the subject that had been on her mind. "What do you think if I were to talk to Mr. Crawford about working in the department store in town a few days a week?"

Most men in the community would be too egotistical to have their wife work outside the home, but she knew Elbert didn't think like most men. There was a pause, and he responded, "That might not be a bad idea."

Martha knew he was smart enough to realize that she didn't make idle remarks; if she had asked the question, she probably had pretty much made up her mind. He knew her well enough to realize she wasn't coy and didn't play games. Besides, he was probably thinking a little extra income never hurt anything. Fortunately for her, Elbert was easygoing and had a "live-and-let-live" philosophy. She didn't restrict him, and he didn't do that to her either.

Martha had learned to drive the car, and she saw no reason she couldn't drive herself to town to talk to Mr. Crawford about a job. Ever the gentleman, Elbert thought he should take her, but again he didn't argue with her plan to go by herself on Monday. She figured the store would be too busy on the weekend.

Bright and early, she walked into the department store and saw the rows of tables with clothing neatly folded on each one. Stacks of shirts, socks, ties, pants and jackets hung by size. There were racks of shoes of every kind. On the ladies' side of the store were hats on various heights of molded heads, shoes arranged according to style, and dresses lined up in built-in alcoves. The unmentionables were kept in cubbyholes underneath the tables. When she entered the store, there was a unique smell, like fresh fabric.

As soon as she entered, a saleslady approached her, "May I help you?" no doubt expecting the ubiquitous response, "No thanks, I'm just looking."

However, what the saleslady got was, "I would like to speak with Mr. Crawford, please." A little startled, the wide-eyed clerk told Martha that he was in the back of the store.

As Martha made her way to the back, she heard the saleslady say to her colleague, "Country girl looking for a job."

Full of the self-confidence of a firstborn, Martha squared her shoulders and said, "Excuse me, sir, Mr. Crawford."

With his spectacles askew, the owner looked up from his books. He recognized this girl but couldn't place her.

Seeing his lack of recognition, she said, "I'm Martha Dalton, well, Martha Hall now. I used to see you when you stopped by our country store on the Batesville Highway. You invited me to come into your store...."

"Oh, yes, the size 8 girl. I do remember you. When I used to come through after being in the Atlanta market!" He had a broad smile. "So, what can I do for you?"

"I've come to inquire about a job." But then, she realized she might have been too blunt and held her breath.

He leaned back in his chair and tapped a pencil on the desk. "Well, what makes you think you have what it takes to work in merchandising?"

Martha hadn't expected this, but she was a quick thinker. "I have experience selling to all kinds of people who stopped at our store, some of them salesmen themselves! So I know how to talk to people. I am not too shy but still respectful. And I love clothes. I'm a good seamstress; my mama taught me." Then, dipping her head a little more shyly, she said, "I think I have a good sense of fashion, what styles and colors look good on people."

She suspected he could sense her discomfort as he looked her up and down. Finally, he stood up and walked around her, commenting on her body type and what she was wearing.

"Hmmm, nice wide shoulders, small waist, with flair to the hips. Tailored clothes, nothing frilly. You should wear heels instead of those oxfords. Show off your ankles. I can see you are not the flirty type, but you may have to learn how to compliment people; it's part of salesmanship. But then again, some of my customers will like your straightforward, direct approach. Yes, you have that country girl innocence."

She jerked her head up; he was beginning to be insulting.

"Now, don't take offense," he continued. "People will see your polite manner. They will know you will be scrupulously honest, not sell them something that isn't suited." He lowered his voice to almost inaudible. "And not have sticky fingers in the cash register."

She felt like he was almost ready to offer her the job when he said, "I don't need another sales girl just now, but I could use a good seamstress. Most of the clothes people buy—men or women—have to be altered. They don't want to pay extra, so I can't offer you much in terms of wages, but I will give you a try to see how it goes. In the back, you can study the stock and how we organize things. You can help find the right size when people see something out front that they like. In the meantime, if we get rushed, you can try your hand at sales. Things are slow during the week, so let's start with Saturdays only."

She left, overjoyed as she headed back to the farm. Then, suddenly, her glee faded as she realized she had not asked about the wages; Elbert would laugh at her for that, but she didn't care. She felt like she was starting her career!

Martha knew Mama would disapprove. She would think a farmer's wife should stay on the farm. Well, her generation was different, and Mama would just have to get used to it.

The first Saturday in the store was pretty busy. The sewing space was located in the stockroom at the back of the store. Fortunately, the sewing machine was underneath a large window. So she had good light and a view of the outside, which made the otherwise stuffy stockroom bearable.

Mr. Crawford would bring the men back to the stockroom for her to pin the alterations that needed to be made. The saleswomen would call her to the front for ladies' alterations in the dressing rooms. Mr. Crawford was always complimentary of her work, but the saleswomen treated her as inferior to them.

Martha could see the organization of other merchandise in the stockroom. For women's wear, they generally put smaller-sized dresses and shoes out front to entice the customers. They would come to the back to get the larger sizes as needed. Mr. Crawford always smiled at Martha and gave her a cheery greeting when he came in the back to retrieve merchandise.

It was a busy Saturday morning, and Martha already had three alterations to be completed by noon. She was busy concentrating and pinning when she felt hands on her shoulders, and they began kneading her shoulders and upper arms.

"Poor Martha, you have to stay hunched over that sewing machine. You need a little massage," Mr. Crawford said in a soft, caressing voice.

She could smell his cologne and feel the warm minty mist of his breath. Martha froze, but Mr. Crawford didn't seem to sense her displeasure, or had he chosen to ignore it? She wasn't sure how she should respond—if she should say something or simply stay quiet.

Just then, Emma, one of the saleswomen, came in. Mr. Crawford removed his hands quickly and said, "Yes, you are right, Martha. Just an inch is needed at the waist." He reverted to being businesslike and moved out front.

All day, Martha winced when anyone came in the back before she could see who it was. Mr. Crawford returned several times, humming a cheery tune, but he seemed to pay no attention to Martha. Nevertheless, she ruminated on the incident all day.

Was it just a simple show of compassion for a fellow worker, or was it a test of something more alarming? She argued with herself like a high school debater. At any rate, she decided not to make a mountain out of a molehill but also to be wary. Wasn't it the girl's responsibility not to put herself in a position for a man to misbehave?

Chapter 27

LYDIA GETS BAD NEWS

"Who did you invite to the pinning ceremony next month, Lydia?" Lily Jane asked. "Are all your siblings coming to see big sister become a real nurse?"

"Goodness, I hope not. There are so many they would take up every seat in the chapel. I think Mama and Papa are coming, and maybe Martha."

"You didn't invite Walter?"

"No, he lives in Florida, remember?"

"It's been a lot of hard work in the last six months, but we made it. The clinical work should be more interesting than the classes, but I'm not looking forward to night duty," said Lily Jane.

With the pinning ceremony only weeks away, Lydia was eager to reach the next milestone. She was on her feet all day and was tired at the end of her shift. She had hurt her back helping a patient get out of bed, and her supervisor had insisted she go to the infirmary. The nurse took a blood sample there, told her to take aspirin if the pain persisted, and said to come back in a week to see the doctor. Lydia was on "light duty" until then. Unfortunately, she continued to have pain, and in fact, it seemed to be getting worse. Lily Jane had insisted she go back to see the doctor.

She hated being in the infirmary, having to take her clothes off and wear this flimsy, floppy gown with only one tie in the back. Time seemed interminable as she sat on the paper sheet on the cold exam table with her feet dangling. *Hurry up*, she thought. *Check my knee reflex, test for sciatica, and give me the prescription.* Her pharmacology professor had once said that a cocktail was as good as a muscle relaxant for back tension. It was apparent he took his own advice. Miss Marshall had taught them that the newest treatment was using ice instead of heat on muscles in spasm.

There was a slight knock on the door, and without waiting for a response, the door opened. The doctor was young—as young as she. He had dark curly hair and a broad face. His eyes were a non-distinct color. He was handsome with a serious look. She noted he had on a wedding band.

"Your bloodwork doesn't look right. I think we need an x-ray. You can get that today. I'll give you some pills to relax the muscles and ease the pain. Come back in a week."

With that, he was gone. No chitchat, this one. Lydia surmised he was a greenhorn trying to look like a wise, busy, and seasoned professional.

The following week passed quickly with the hectic pace of a student nurse's life. She took the pain pill only at bedtime and was officially still on "light duty" until released by the doctor. So she tried to minimize any work requiring a strong back. She even asked for help getting Mr. Banner up and into the wheelchair.

She made it back to the infirmary late in the day. She hoped the x-ray didn't show anything wrong with her vertebrae and that she needed only to wait for the strained muscle to heal. Then, maybe they would change "light duty" to "days off," and she would get an excuse to lie in bed for a few days. But wouldn't that chafe Lily Jane, who also hated the early morning hours?

Again, it was an interminable wait on the cold exam table. Was he saving her until last—not making the paying patients wait? Finally, there was a brief knock as the door opened. His face showed concern, probably due to a long and frustrating day. He kept looking at the chart and not at her. He stammered around, talking about bloodwork and her general health.

Then came the fateful words, "The x-ray showed a mass on the left kidney."

She stared at him, not believing what she had heard. Denial set in. "Maybe a shadow?"

"We sent it to Columbus to a kidney specialist. He says it's definitely a mass." He hastened to add, "But not all masses are cancer. Some are harmless fatty tumors. But still, they have to be removed. Maybe the entire kidney has to be removed. But people can live fine with just one kidney."

All his words ran together, and she heard them like a distant echo. It felt like a blow with a 2 x 4. Lydia couldn't take it in. There must be a mistake.

"I just wrenched my back! I thought it would be healed by now." She knew she was screeching.

"Well, that may be true, but you definitely have a kidney mass. Here, look at the x-ray. There's no mistake."

Lydia lay back on the exam table and squeezed her eyes closed. Then, turning on her side, she curled up in a ball. She would escape this nonsense, gladly put on her uniform, and get up early for work tomorrow. After all, she was too young to have a mass and certainly too young and healthy to have cancer.

"You had better talk this over with your family. I will give you the name of the doctor in Columbus. He'd be the best one to do the surgery. I don't know how long you'd need for recovery, but you should be able to arrange a leave of absence with the school."

She felt so angry, she wanted to hit him. Advising her to ruin her life, crush all her dreams, and make her an invalid when she was so close to achieving freedom and a life of exciting adventures. *No, no, no.* This could not be her reality. The anger suddenly left, and she felt like a puddle of melted butter. Utterly bereft.

She barely heard the doctor's words, who told her to wait here, as he left the room. She couldn't have moved, anyway. She wasn't sure how long she stayed there but she heard the door open, and one of her instructors entered the room. Miss Grogan hugged her and then gently helped her get dressed.

"You will come to my office. We will get in touch with your family and make a plan. God will see you through this, Lydia. You are a strong young woman."

"No, I'm not," Lydia cried. "I can't do this. Why, why, why?"

That night, she tore the page in her journal, bearing down so hard, her hand expressing the fury she felt. She even wrote some choice words she once heard a surgeon use when the scrub nurse wasn't quick enough to pass him an instrument—Damn! Hell! Shit!

The surgery had gone well, the doctors said. The pathology report showed it was a lipoma. Lydia couldn't even be thankful it wasn't cancer; her life was over anyway. She would be an invalid at a young age, destined to live at home with Mama and her young siblings. She had lost all enthusiasm for life. Mama was quoting all kinds of Bible verses to her, but Lydia tuned her out. Everyone tried to encourage her, but it was easier to give in and accept her unhappiness. She was mad at the world.

Lily Jane had visited and tried to give her a pep talk. "You will be healed in no time. And then you can come back to school. I'll make sure ol' Marshall assigns you only easy patients from now on."

Lydia tried to elicit a smile. "I don't plan to come back to school. What if something happens to my other kidney? Or there are lipomas in other places in my body? No, from now on, I will only look after myself. I didn't really like nursing all that much, anyway. Wiping people's butts. There are no cute doctors at our hospital; they must all go to the big city."

"Well, what are you going to do with the rest of your life? You are too young to give up."

Lydia didn't respond, but later she rolled her thoughts over in her mind before she recorded them in her journal. *Be practical. Being an invalid is not such a bad deal. Everyone waits on me, hand and foot. If I can't live life, I'll just lie in bed with a good book and live a fantasy life. After all, this is so unfair to me! Why shouldn't I be selfish?*

Mama came into her "sick room," as Lydia had begun to call her bedroom. She was propped up on fluffy pillows reading a book Martha had brought her.

"There's someone here to see you, Lydia."

Lydia faked a smile. The endless number of cousins and other long-lost relatives came in a steady stream to see the girl whose life had been ruined. Doing their duty to bring her a bit of cheer and then return to their busy lives, thanking God it wasn't them. Then, she first saw his shoes—the shiny black ones she would know anywhere. "Walter!" she exclaimed with genuine surprise.

"You are the hardest person to find! Every time I go to where you were the last time, they tell me you are somewhere different," he said with a teasing smile, hat in his hand but dressed to the nines in his business suit.

Mama had come into the room with him. Lord knows, a bedridden invalid needed a chaperone. Lydia introduced them, although he had introduced himself when Mama answered the door.

Turning serious, he said, "I was sorry to hear about your surgery. I saw Lily Jane when I went to the nursing school to call on you. She said it turned out okay, but that you were home recovering. I brought you something from my last trip. I know how you love to read, and this is all the rage in Atlanta." He gave her a beautifully bound book of *Gone with the Wind.*

"We like to read the Bible in this household," commented Mama. Lydia, embarrassed at the lack of appreciation in Mama's comment, compensated with ebullient thanks.

"I'll think of you every time I read it." She saw the scowl on Mama's face, but she didn't care.

"Well, I don't want to tire you, so I'll be on my way. I'll be back this way in a couple of weeks, and I'd like to stop again and see how you are progressing."

Before Mama could respond, Lydia chimed in, "That would be nice. Your visit has cheered me up so much, and thank you for this lovely gift. I shall treasure it."

True to his word, Walter was back in two weeks. He was happy to see Lydia in a chair, gaining a little more strength. "I think what you need is a little Florida sunshine."

That got Mama's attention, and her hackles up. "You and your mother could ride back with me. I have an extra bedroom. My mother lives with me, and I have a housekeeper. The house has a veranda—an indoor porch where you can get the sunlight and warmth, but not the direct heat. It would be very good for recuperating."

It was the first excitement Lydia had felt since the surgery. And she secretly laughed at the shocked expression on Mama's face.

"What a generous invitation. We will think about it," Lydia responded before Mama could speak.

Chapter 28

MARTHA'S SURPRISE INVITATION

M artha was pleased to have Phoebe come to visit her and Elbert. All her siblings loved a chance to go to the Hall Farm for a few days. She knew Phoebe would want to hear all about her job at the department store.

"Do you think you could help me get a job in town?" Phoebe asked. "Money is getting tight at home; Papa doesn't seem to have as much energy as he used to, and James is working his own farm as well as trying to help Papa. We could use the extra income."

"I could help you apply for a salesgirl's job at the Five and Dime," Martha offered.

Phoebe asked Martha what it was like working at the Crawford Department Store as the two girls sat on the front porch with glasses of sweet tea.

"I absolutely love it! Since I am working full time, I have learned the big picture—monitoring the inventory, displaying merchandise, and making the sale. The only thing I haven't had a chance to do is see the bookkeeping system. But I know the basics from working at our own store. I would love to go to Atlanta on a buying trip one day. See how decisions are made about upcoming fashion trends. Of course, I am still doing alterations at the store, but that, too, is informative—the right length of dresses for your body type, how to camouflage rounded shoulders and pooches in front." Martha's enthusiasm showed.

Phoebe was curious and not afraid to ask personal questions. "What does Elbert think about your working, like having a *career*?"

"At first, he wasn't too keen on it, but he didn't say so. I suspect he worried that others would think he couldn't support me—that I had to work outside the home. But Elbert is more open than most men. Besides, he knows he'd best not stand in my way when I make up my mind to do something." They both laughed.

Martha looked out over the pasture as she continued. "Neither of us planned to live on a farm. He has always wanted to own a grocery store in town, and as soon as we can turn this farm over to somebody else, he will start living his dream."

Phoebe didn't hesitate to pry. "I suppose then you will have to quit your job at the department store to help him."

Martha sighed. "That's what he wants, but I love what I do. The garment industry is so much more interesting than the produce industry." They both laughed again.

"Since the store is open every day but Sunday, do you get tired of going to work six days a week?" Phoebe asked with all sincerity.

Martha laughed, "It's better than the farm—seven days a week. The worst part is leaving Mattie, but she loves being with her Daddy and Grandma Lucille, and I know Flossie spoils her. Flossie is like a member of the family. She does all my housework and has supper ready in the evening. I love my life, except I'd rather live in town."

On a Thursday morning, while Martha was altering a dress for one of the customers, Mr. Crawford came to the back to ask when she would be done.

"In one minute. I'm on the last few inches of this hem."

"Then I will wait," he said, pulling up a chair.

"You are such an asset to the store, Martha," he said. She looked up, startled at the remark. "Why, thank you."

"I mean it. You have a natural talent, and you relate well to the customers. You have something my other salesgirls lack—maybe it is sincerity—and customers can tell you want them to look good.

You're not just trying to make a sale. That is a key factor in long-term success. That is what keeps customers coming back."

Martha was blushing by now, but his remarks validated how she felt about her abilities.

"I appreciate that, Mr. Crawford."

"Oh, I think we are past being so formal. Please call me Sam." He had always called her Martha.

She stumbled as she said, "Oh, I don't think I can do that, Mr. Crawford." He was old enough to be her father, and it seemed impolite. However, she didn't want to offend him.

"How about if I call you Mr. Sam?"

"That's what you call old people! No. Just Sam. I'd like us to be on intimate terms. In fact, I'd like to groom you to take on a larger role in the store. I think you could one day be the Assistant Manager."

Martha felt a flutter in her stomach when she heard "intimate," but decided he hadn't meant it romantically, but only that they should think of each other as peers, business friends if not quite equals. She could see herself in the role of manager. She already knew things she would do to improve business. His vision for her was almost too good to be true.

"Would you be willing to do what it takes to be Assistant Manager?" His eyes bored into hers.

"Oh yes! And I appreciate the opportunity. Just guide me to what I need to learn."

He patted her lightly on the shoulders as he left her to finish the sewing.

It was the following week when Martha got the surprise of her life. Sam asked if she wanted to go to the Atlanta Mart with him in two weeks. He hastened to explain that his wife was also going. They would be gone three days to the Apparel Show and select merchandise for the next season. They would stay in a hotel, and she would have a room all to herself, order room service, and pamper herself, he said. She was so excited and accepted right away before even discussing it with Elbert. However, that evening, she could see Elbert had some reservations.

"Why you? Why not one of the salesgirls? I'd think they would have more experience knowing what ladies will like."

"Mr. Crawford wants me to learn every aspect of the business so I can one day take on more management responsibilities." She had decided not to say anything about a future Assistant Manager role to avoid jinxing that goal.

"His wife is going? But she won't be making the rounds at the Mart, will she? So it will be just you and Mr. Crawford?

"Just me and Mr. Crawford and a few thousand other people at the Mart."

"Well, I trust your judgment. And I hope you have a good time."

"I'm going to pay Grannie a visit to brush up on fancy dining—you know, which fork to use when," Martha said with a raised eyebrow.

Martha had not bothered to call ahead, but she knocked lightly on the screen door and let herself in. Grannie Chambers, her maternal grandmother, was getting hard of hearing. Still, since she always welcomed anyone into the parsonage, the door was never locked. Martha found her in her usual spot— in the sunroom in the white wicker rocker with chintz-covered pillows. The west sun streaming in gave the best light for darning black socks. Looking at her from the back, Martha smiled at the elaborate Gibson girl hairdo Grannie styled every day. She might be a small town preacher's wife, but she never lost her taste for glamour.

"Oh, Martha, what a nice surprise! Come in, child."

Giving her a cheek kiss, Martha hastened to explain that she couldn't stay long, but she needed help. She watched Grannie's eyes widen, and her brows rise up with alarm.

"Oh, there's nothing wrong. It's a good thing. I've been invited to go to Atlanta on a merchandising trip with Mr. and Mrs. Crawford. You know I've never been to fancy restaurants before. I think I need some coaching. I don't want to embarrass myself."

"Now I know my Betts taught you good manners."

"Yes, but I need a refresher and maybe an advanced course," Martha said with a mischievous grin.

Grannie gave a self-assured smile. "Okay, I'll give you the works. I hear there is a new book coming out by Miss Emily Post about etiquette, but I know everything there is to know about fancy dinners. I've been to so many Baptist Convention banquets I can't count them all. Now, let's talk about some basics first."

"Let the gentleman pull the chair out for you and thank him as you sit. First thing, unfold your napkin and put it in your lap, although sometimes, in fancy places, the waiter does it for you. Always be gracious and thank the waiter for anything he does.

The silverware utensils in the outermost positions are to be used first and in order, working inward toward the plate. Never start eating until your hostess does. When you pause during eating but have not finished, place your utensils on the side of the plate---knife on the right, fork on the left. When you have completed your meal, put your silverware straight up and down in the middle of the plate.

The correct way to eat bread is to first use your knife to put a bit of butter on the side of your bread plate. Then tear off a bite-sized piece, butter it, and eat it. Do this one bite at a time. Also, cut your meat one bite at a time.

"Now for the Don'ts. Don't tuck your napkin into your blouse. Don't put your elbows on the table. Don't scrape your plate or sop your bread. Don't put used silverware back on the table. Place the spoon on the saucer if you stir your coffee with a spoon. Don't start dessert until the hostess or everyone else does."

"What about a cocktail or wine? All we have ever had is homemade wine." Martha was hesitant to ask, but this was her only chance. She need not have worried. Grannie didn't flinch.

"The gentleman may suggest the alcoholic beverage. If not, a good generic cocktail is the Tom Collins, but don't tell Grandpa I know about such things!" she said with a conspiratorial laugh.

"Either the gentleman or the waiter will suggest a wine with dinner. You won't have to worry about that. The waiter will usually pour a tiny bit for the gentleman to taste. If he nods his approval, the waiter will serve the ladies first. After everyone has been served, the host may make a toast. If not, the way to start your wine is in three steps.

"First, keep the glass on the table, but gently swirl it. Next, you raise it to your nose to experience the bouquet. Only then do you take a sip. You will find that many people comment on the wine's taste after the first sip. 'Nice and oaky,' or since you don't know much about wines, just say 'it's pleasant.'"

"Thanks, Grannie. I know I will be nervous, but I will try to act like I eat this way every day at home!"

"Simply relax and be yourself. Experience the delight of an elegant dinner. Now, tell me all about how this trip came about and what you will be doing."

Chapter 29

MARTHA AND THE MART

The big day arrived, and Elbert drove Martha to the store early Tuesday morning. "I hope I didn't forget to pack anything." Despite her careful preparation, Martha was nervous.

"If you forgot something, you'll be at a good place to shop," Elbert joked.

The plan was that after Sam opened the store and took care of a few things, they would leave for Atlanta. When Martha entered the store, she found she had one alteration she needed to finish while Sam instructed the senior girl who would be in charge for the next three days. Sam loaded her suitcase when all was in order, and they headed out of town. Martha was surprised that he drove straight for the highway.

"Aren't we picking up your wife?"

"Oh, I forgot to tell you. She went up yesterday with her brother so she could spend an extra day with her sister who lives in Atlanta."

With a small amount of trepidation, Martha tried to relax. As they drove in silence on the way out of town, she chastised herself for being worried. They passed by Martha's homestead and the small grocery store where Mr. Crawford had first met Martha.

"We would stop and see your folks, but we need to get to Atlanta in time to go to this evening's opening of the Mart."

Martha relayed that everyone was doing well. She told him about her brother and his wife expecting their second baby. The only sad news was about Lydia's surgery and her dropping out of nursing school. He was very sympathetic.

"Now, Martha, I want you to be alert to the changes in fashion. We may be a small town, but our ladies deserve to look as good as any Parisian. On the other hand, we don't want to shock our customers with something drastically different. No one wants to be the first to strike out with something outrageous."

She responded, "I've noticed the difference in taste in the generations. Younger girls are more likely to try a new style. But a lot of our older customers seem to buy the same thing over and over." She enjoyed sharing her observations. This felt like a professional conversation.

"Yes, but it's our job to keep them fashionable, so people will ask them where they got such a lovely outfit. We have a big responsibility to make women feel they are beautiful." He looked over and smiled at her.

They continued with this kind of business talk, and Martha relaxed and enjoyed the trip.

They made a rest stop after driving about halfway. Martha was aware that other travelers stared at them with curiosity as if they were wondering if they were a May-December married couple on a trip. She felt embarrassed.

She had been to Atlanta only once with Grandpa and Grannie Chambers when she was about six years old. She enjoyed the scenery of the trip and got more and more excited. As they approached the city, traffic grew heavier, and the forest and fields of the country were replaced by building after building. She jumped at a loud noise and turned to see a semi-truck impatient to get around them. *Things move at a different pace here*, she thought.

When they arrived at the hotel, Sam expressed dismay that his wife, Ruth, wasn't there yet.

"She was supposed to have her brother bring her to the hotel and have her check in before we arrived. I'll find out what the trouble is as soon as I get in the room."

Sam made plans for the three of them to meet in the hotel dining room for dinner, and then he and Martha would head across the street to the Mart.

Martha was in the room next to them. Her room was lovely, with the bedspread and draperies matching in a sophisticated combination of yellow, black, and gray. It was indeed the most luxurious bedroom she'd ever stayed in. She had an hour before dinner and decided to take a relaxing soak in the tub and a quick rest.

"If Mama and the girls could see me now!" She liked this lifestyle and once again let herself envision her future as an Assistant Manager, making trips like this to Atlanta and maybe someday even New York.

Martha was prompt for the dinner engagement but was puzzled to see Sam sitting alone at a table for two. He quickly explained.

"Ruth's sister has come down with a fever, and she decided to stay another night with her. Since we will spend most of the evening at the Mart, it's just as well that she won't have to be alone in a hotel room tonight." This was readily understandable, but Martha got another uneasy feeling. She worried about the *May-December* perception she saw in other patrons' faces.

The Atlanta Mart was the most exciting place Martha had ever been. The wholesale trade center was in a four-story warehouse-type building. There seemed to be hundreds of vendors in the Apparel Show featuring ready-to-wear. Merchants wandered at will, previewing goods that claimed to predict what next season's fashions and fads would be. Vendors offered drinks and sitting areas to entice merchants to stop, visit, and peruse their wares.

Dresses, hats, shoes, coats, accessories—it was a shopper's paradise. The salesmen explained that the Flapper age influenced this year's fashions. Martha was surprised but pleased to learn that corsets were gone. Dress styles had changed from mid-calf to below-the-knee, and fitted waists were passé. Dresses now had a drop waist and were loose and straight. Popular shoes were Mary Janes with a T-strap with heels. Pumps had bows.

She wasn't sure if her lady customers would go so far as to wear the fedoras or newsboy hats but would probably like the cloche hats. Coats had a fur trim. Fringe wraps were in. This was her world, and she could not remember being happier!

They had each taken a notebook to record what they wanted to order; they shared opinions, and she was pleased Sam valued her thoughts. She had wondered about mark-ups and calculated that the merchant generally placed the sales price at 2.5 times the wholesale cost. No wonder merchants did so well!

The evening passed quickly, and she was exhausted when they arrived back at the hotel. They agreed on a time to meet for breakfast. Then they would return to the Mart for a full day of exploring what the creative manufacturers were offering. Martha listened as Sam told her, "You have to exercise discipline—you can't buy everything that appeals to you. Your purchases need to be guided by a smart guess at what would sell to your local customers."

Martha nodded her understanding and said, "I've been overwhelmed with the changes in fashion, but I think it best to tour the whole Mart before deciding. I don't want to be enticed by things that first caught my eye. I need to think about our customers. I can see how this is a hard job every year."

Her excitement was evident to Elbert when she telephoned that night. He said he was glad she was enjoying the experience, but she noted an edge to his voice. He didn't like farming and was frustrated that this role had been thrust upon him. He told Martha he had looked again at real estate in town, but everything had gotten more expensive. With the sadness in his voice, she decided she'd better tone down her enthusiasm and change the subject.

"How are Mattie and Miss Lucille?"

At breakfast, Martha inquired about Ruth's sister and learned that she was better, and Ruth was expected at the hotel by noon. Even though lunch would be available at the Mart, Sam planned to meet Ruth for lunch at the hotel. Martha would be on her own for an hour or so. She felt entirely confident shopping by herself. As she did so that afternoon, she was treated with great respect and envisioned herself having her own store and running her own business someday.

That evening at dinner, Martha met Ruth and inquired about her sister.

"I'm worried about her. She is not well and has lost much weight since I last saw her. I think I have convinced her she must see a doctor to get a thorough check-up."

They enjoyed a glass of wine, and Martha reported on her afternoon of visiting vendors. The only wines Martha had ever had were the homemade Scuppernong and Muscadine wines Papa fermented from the grapes on the backyard arbor. There was no comparison with the wine they were now drinking— so smooth and without the Georgia grapes' sharp taste. She could get used to these California wines. Sam knew the right wine to order with the entrée. As Martha watched the interaction between Ruth and Sam, she noted he was very considerate of her, and she seemed to dote on him. A happy marriage was a pleasure to witness. And Martha relaxed.

The plan for the third day was to get an early start at the Mart and complete the shopping by four o'clock that afternoon and then head home. Martha was more enamored with her career than ever.

Chapter 30

MARTHA'S CRISIS

Three months later, the merchandise they had selected at the Mart began to arrive. Martha directed the salesgirls to unpack and ready things to be displayed to the best advantage. They had all come to accept that Martha was the day-to-day operations manager. Mr. Crawford spent more time at his desk in the back with paperwork—especially when Martha was back there doing alterations.

Martha still did all the tailoring but was out front during the busy time of the day. She knew they would soon need another seamstress and hoped she could recommend one of her sisters.

Business always waned near the end of the day. The silence was broken by the phone ringing in the back room. It was unusual to get calls at the store. Mainly, the phone was used for Mr. Crawford to make calls. Martha and the girls could hear his voice but not the words. He sounded upset, and they looked at each other with puzzled frowns. After the call, silence resumed. They hadn't expected an explanation, but the longer the silence continued, the more curious they all were.

After about ten minutes, Mr. Crawford came out of the back. He said, "My wife's sister in Atlanta has died unexpectedly. I am going home to be with her and make plans to travel. Carry on as usual, and I'll get in touch with you as soon as possible. I'll probably close the store for a couple of days when a decision is made about the funeral service. Martha, I'm leaving you in charge until I get back."

"Yes, sir, and I am so sorry for your loss. I know how fond Mrs. Crawford was of her sister. If there is anything I can do, please let me know."

Sam looked at her and replied, "I'm counting on you."

The other girls murmured their condolences as well, and Mr. Crawford went out the back door and got into his car.

Within an hour, Mr. Crawford came back and seemed much calmer. He told the girls he had ordered a black wreath to be put on the store door, with a sign that the store would be closed for the next two days and open again on Monday.

"Martha, please choose a couple of black dresses for my wife to wear. She is too distraught to come into the store. I will take them to the house. I know it is a lot to ask of you, Martha, but would you mind terribly coming to the house with your sewing kit in case alterations need to be made?"

"I would be happy to," she replied.

"And plan to drive your car, so you can go home from there. Hopefully, we won't take too much of your time."

"Time is no problem. Just let me call Elbert so he won't worry if I'm late."

Elbert expressed his sympathy and told Martha not to worry about time.

"In fact, I will be gone myself until late this evening, and I may have a surprise for you."

Martha thought it unwise to have any enthusiasm or curiosity in her voice, so she kept her tone flat and the conversation short.

"And the others of you can go ahead and leave, and I will lock up the store," said Mr. Crawford. He seemed calm and in control of things.

Martha knew where Sam and Ruth lived. All the houses on the street except the Crawford's were Southern plantation-style homes with big porches and fluted columns. The Crawford house was plain white brick with no porch at all. It seemed to suggest a preference for privacy, with nothing inviting about it.

The house was only one story but large, covering the whole lot with very little grass and no flowers. The garage was on the side, and Martha saw Sam waiting for her to pull into the driveway. He ushered her to park in the empty space beside his car. As she was getting out, she was surprised that he had closed the garage door as she didn't expect to stay very long. She felt slightly claustrophobic.

"Get your sewing kit and come through the back door," Sam said in a very businesslike tone.

Martha did as she was told and excused his abruptness based on his sad shock and concern for his wife. He was darting about like a skittish rabbit when they entered the kitchen.

"Let me take these dresses back to the bedroom. Please make yourself comfortable in the living room," he said as he ushered her into a beautifully decorated room.

There was a rich, colorful Aubusson rug on the floor, the kind she had seen in magazines. It gave the room an air of foreign elegance; she was sure it had not come from the local furniture stores. Perhaps he had bought it in New York, a place she could only imagine. The curtains were drawn, but a few accent lamps were on, giving the place a mysterious feel.

In a few minutes, Sam was back. "Ahhh, it seems Ruth has gone out. She left a note that she would be back in a few minutes."

Again, Martha was surprised but accepted that the crisis was causing both Sam and Ruth to have muddled thinking.

"I need a drink to calm my nerves," Sam said as he opened the cabinet of a beautiful piece of furniture.

"What will you have, Martha?"

"Oh, nothing for me, thanks." Martha was getting frustrated; she had expected to be on her way home soon.

"I will get you some iced tea from the kitchen. I don't want to drink alone."

He was gone for a few minutes and returned with a crystal goblet of iced tea. She wasn't sure what he was drinking, but it smelled like bourbon—not a wise idea for someone who anticipated driving to Atlanta shortly.

Sam sat but got up a minute later, went to the Victrola, and put on a record of Glenn Miller. The music was slow and dreamy and matched the atmosphere of the dimly lighted room.

How strange, thought Martha. She sat on the edge of her seat, unsure what to say, so she drank her iced tea in silence.

Sam downed the rest of his drink and went to pour another.

"Well, while we are waiting on Ruth, why don't I give you a tour of the house? Then you can choose which room has the best light for fitting Ruth's dress."

Martha was uncomfortable wandering through the house like this, and she felt a little dizzy, but she didn't see what choice she had. The dark hallway had beautiful polished mahogany floors, and the walls had portraits of what must have been their ancestors. She didn't think it proper to linger or to ask questions.

The first room off the hall was a library with a comfortable-looking leather chair and an antique desk. Next to it was what Sam referred to as the powder room. At the end of the hall was an enormous bedroom; the bed cover was moiré silk, and there was a boudoir chair covered in the same material. A six-foot tall armoire with mirrored doors stood against the other wall. She could see an adjoining bathroom with a marble counter and gold fixtures.

"This is Ruth's bedroom."

Martha bit her tongue before revealing her surprise and responding, "Ruth's bedroom?"

Sam took her elbow and turned her toward the hall.

"And across the hall is my bedroom." He kept a hand on her elbow as he made sure she went through the doorway. She heard the door shut and the lock turn.

"Aahh, Martha, I need some comfort," he softly said.

Martha panicked, no longer in doubt of what he had on his mind and chastised herself for being so gullible. But Sam? Her boss?

"I must go," Martha said, turning toward the door.

Sam blocked her way. "But you extended your sympathies and asked if there was anything you could do to help. You can help me! I need affection."

"I'm sorry you misunderstood. I must leave now." She again tried to get around him to the door.

"Martha, Martha, Martha." His voice was strident now. "I told you I would make you Assistant Manager, and I asked you if you would be willing to do what it takes, and you said 'yes.' Well, this is what it takes. You must be nice to the boss!" He laughed a gloomy laugh.

"Mr. Crawford, move out of my way. Now!"

Her anger seemed to increase his own. He grabbed her by the shoulders, and she was shocked at his strength. He pushed her backward, and she lost her balance. Suddenly he had her flat on the bed and was pulling on her blouse.

Seeing how her anger affected him, she tried to soften her voice, "Now, Sam, I know you are not yourself. Ruth will be coming back any minute, and you wouldn't want her to see you this upset."

"Oh, but she's not coming back. She is already on her way to Atlanta. Her brother from Cordelia came by to pick her up. I'm not going until tomorrow, and our time together will be our little secret. You don't know how many times I have dreamed of this moment, Martha."

He gritted his teeth and mustered more strength as he continued to jerk up her skirt and pull at her underpants. She fought with all her might, clawed at his face leering down at her, twisted to escape him, but to no avail. As she was kicking him, she knew she was also bashing her dream and all hopes of a career.

He hit her hard in the stomach, knocking the breath out of her, and she went limp. The assault lasted only a few minutes, but it changed a lifetime. When he unlocked and opened the door, she was vaguely aware of the record stuck on the Victrola.

Chapter 31

MARTHA SEEKS COMFORT

She was crying so hard she could barely see to drive. All Martha knew was she had to get away. She thought about the sewing kit she had left behind. It had her favorite thimble. Damn him, and damn the sewing kit! She never wanted to see either again.

The adrenaline pumped through her body as her mind raced, thinking about what to do. What if she went to the police? She would only embarrass herself and would never live down the stigma. On the other hand, if she told Elbert, there was no telling what he would do to Sam, and he wouldn't care about the consequences. Or he might even blame her or never want to touch her again. She would be disgraced.

And the family—Mama would never get over it. Papa would hurt so badly for her. Everyone would pity her. One thing is for sure—she could never go back to work in that store. Her dreams were dashed.

She had worked so hard and loved being at the store. Now she felt angry, sad, furious, and afraid—all mixed together.

"Damn it all to hell," she yelled as she hit the steering wheel with her fist.

She couldn't go home with her blouse torn and as disheveled as she was. But Elbert would be worried that she was so late. Then, it came to her in a flash; she would go to James, who lived not too far from here. James was not as hot-headed as Elbert, and he would help her think through what to do. She could call Elbert from there and tell him she went to check on Sally Ann, whose baby was due pretty soon. Her breathing slowed as she calmed down with this plan.

But as she drove on, she suddenly was unsure she would be welcome at James' home with this problem. The family had not treated him well after the shotgun wedding. What if he scoffed at her and told her she was asking for it by working in town? Now she would be the family outcast. But nevertheless, she would have to take that chance. She could not go home in this state.

When she stopped at the house, she could see James' truck was gone, but a light was on. She didn't know what she would do if they were gone, but just then, the door opened, and Sally Ann flashed her a welcoming smile.

"You just missed James. He and Louis left to take a tractor part he repaired back to...." She stopped mid-sentence when she saw how distraught Martha was.

"Martha, what in the world happened? Are you all right?"

"No, I'm not all right!" It was such a relief for Martha to share what had happened. She had energy from her anger, and at the same time, she felt like a weak, defeated victim as she related her story.

Without seeming to go anywhere, Sally Ann produced a cup of hot tea with lemon and honey for Martha to drink. She gave her full attention to Martha.

"I can't ever go back in that store, but what will I tell Elbert? I will tell him I've had enough of working long hours and I want to stay home for a change. I will have to convince Elbert and everyone else that I am sincere." Martha asked many questions but would also answer them as Sally Ann sat quietly and listened.

Martha remembered she was going to call Elbert. "Sally Ann, I will have to tell a little white lie, and I hope you will back me up." Then, not waiting for an answer, she said, "I will tell Elbert I came to see about you. How are you doing, anyway?"

"You can tell him I have a terrible backache, my legs are swollen, and...."

As if she hadn't realized Sally Ann was answering her question, Martha interrupted, "God, I have to bathe. I can't stand it. Can you put on some water to boil and get your tub out? I want it scalding hot." Martha then turned and began to dial.

"Hmmm, funny, there's no answer. He told me he was going to be out too and that he would have a surprise for me. I can't imagine what it is. I hope I can fake being pleased with whatever he brings home."

In a calming voice, Sally Ann said, "I'll get the bath ready. Then we will get you fixed up. I have a white blouse similar to yours. Let's trade. Clean your face in the washbowl, then straighten your hair while the tub water is heating."

Martha was taking these instructions and felt herself beginning to calm down. The sooner she bathed, the better. She scrubbed and scrubbed and finally was ready to towel off and get dressed.

Sally Ann had laid out her white blouse and secretly added a clean pair of underpants. When Martha was dressed, Sally Ann said, "Are you sure you feel okay to drive home?"

"Whew, I'm much calmer now. I have to get through this evening. The quicker I can get to bed, the fewer questions asked, the better. And tomorrow is a new day."

When Martha drove into her yard, she saw that Elbert's truck was still gone. She went into the house; all was quiet. She crept down the hall and saw that Mattie was curled up on her grandmother's bed. Miss Lucille was asleep, too, with a fairy tale book fallen to the side. Martha was sorry that Mattie was already asleep because she would have been a distraction. Getting her to bed would have given her a reason not to face Elbert immediately.

Just then she heard the truck drive in and saw the headlights through the front window. She went toward the porch to meet Elbert with her story ready.

Elbert came in with a hang-dog expression. He didn't seem to recognize anything wrong with Martha.

"I didn't get the loan, Martha. So we're stuck here on this farm!"

She moved toward him and gave him a fierce hug, as much for him as for herself.

All weekend, Martha paced the floor and stewed. She cursed under her breath. Sam had taken so much from her—her faith in humanity, her dignity, her ability to be honest with her husband or any of her sisters. She wanted revenge, then couldn't believe she had that thought.

The dirty son-of-a bitch! She was about to burst from holding it all inside. She decided to clean out the kitchen cabinets. Anything to allow her to throw things around and scrub like fury. *I'll make him pay. I'll make him pay for this!*

An idea began to form in her head. Hurt him in the pocketbook. But how? She couldn't blackmail him? Or could she? That would be sweet revenge! Maybe even get enough for Elbert to open the store.

She grinned at the irony of that. But how could she explain where the money came from? *Mr. Crawford has a big heart and wants to help you get a start in your business? No, that would never fly.*

By Monday morning, she had a plan. It would take all the courage she had. She would get the upper hand or else. It took all her willpower to walk into that store, and she deliberately came one hour late.

"Mr. Crawford, I'd like to speak to you in the back." All heads snapped up at the tone of Martha's voice. She headed to the back, and a surprised Mr. Crawford followed her. He had a quizzical expression on his face, not knowing how this would go.

She got close enough to spit on him and snarled, "If you ever so much as lay a pinky finger on me again, I swear I will gouge your eyes out." She stared at him while he blinked. "Now, first of all, you are going to double my salary and name me Assistant Manager, starting today. After that, I will come in and leave whenever I please. Don't ever come in this back room when I am here alone. I can and will ruin you in this town whenever I choose."

"Now, Martha," he said condescendingly.

"No, I'm telling you. You thought I was some sniveling little country girl, didn't you? Well, you don't understand how tough little country girls can be, do you? Shall I raise my voice now, or do we have an agreement?"

He sighed, "I'm sorry; I don't know what came over...."

"Shut up. I don't want to hear it." Her voice went up an octave.

"Okay, okay. Starting today."

"And one more thing, you will loan my husband $500, so he can start a grocery store. I will tell him to come by tomorrow. You can draw up loan papers."

Mr. Crawford's mouth gaped open.

"You will do that because you value me as an employee and want us to be closer to town. Plus, you are a civic-minded businessman and want our community to prosper. You do it all the time, for other people too. To you, it's as good as keeping your money in the bank."

With that, Martha walked out front and smiled at the salesgirls. "Good morning, ladies. Let's get to work making sales."

Elbert was just as surprised as Sam, but Martha did a bang-up job convincing him it was nothing out of the ordinary. They'd borrow from a wealthy businessman instead of the bank. Elbert's brother, Frederick, had found an Army buddy who agreed to live on the farm and help him assume responsibility. Miss Lucille would stay on the farm.

Elbert, Martha and Mattie would move into town and start Hall's Grocery store. Within two weeks of the store opening, Martha quit her job at the department store. But not before reminding Mr. Crawford she was capable of ruining him anytime she chose.

Chapter 32

JAMES AND LOUIS

James drove his old truck, and Louis rode shotgun. They had finished working on the oil pump of Mr. Miller's ancient tractor and returned it after they got off work at the sawmill. He and Louis both had a knack for fixing things, especially machinery. They liked working together; what one couldn't figure out, the other could.

They enjoyed joshing with each other too. That kept James from thinking how miserable his life was, living in a shack and scraping to make ends meet. He knew Louis didn't have it any better. He still lived with his mama, daddy, and four sisters in a small house with three rooms. They, too, had an outhouse. Louis' daddy had a little garden, chickens and a milk cow.

"How much you think we should charge ol' man Miller for the work we done on this oil pump, Louis?"

"He a neighbor, ain't he? We ought not charge him nothin'."

"Oh no, my friend, we gonna charge him. I say four dollars, at least. We'll split it even. Two dollars for you and two dollars for me."

Louis shook his head. "If you give me that much money, I'll just put it in the collection plate next Sunday. Maybe it'll help somebody."

"Are you crazy, man? Spend the money on yourself. You deserve it. Or save it for your future."

"The way I look at it, God's been good to me. We supposed to love our neighbor, treat them like you would treat yourself."

"Now, you soundin' like a preacher, Louis."

"Yeah? Well, lately, I been feelin' like the Lord is calling me to preach."

"Well, don't go preachin' at me. I got enough of that from Mama to last me a lifetime."

"How you doin' with your mama? You back in her good graces? She seen what a sweet daughter-in-law she got?"

"Hell, nah. She's as snooty as ever. One day she will regret the way she's treated us."

"The Good Book say forgive, over and over again if necessary."

"I'll forgive all right. When hell freezes over."

They rode in silence for a while. The spell was broken when they drove into the yard of the Miller farm. True to his word, James got four dollars for fixing the tractor part. He shut off the truck engine when he dropped Louis off at home.

"Think I'll come in and visit with your mama for a little bit, Louis, seein' as I ain't got no mama of my own."

"She'll be glad to see you."

"Hey, Miss Fannie. How you doin'?" James asked.

She was sitting on the porch, shelling peas. James took a seat in the other rocking chair, and Louis went to the back garden where his father was. James had loved Miss Fannie ever since he could remember. She had a sweet, round face. He saw some tiny black moles forming around her eyes. Her smile, with that gap between her front teeth and sparkling brown eyes, told him she was genuinely glad to see him.

When he kissed her on the cheek, he always felt like he was kissing a marshmallow. She had let Louis and James play in the mud or whatever they wanted to do when they were little. She'd clean him up before she sent him home. She had been a second mama.

"You look sad, son. What's the matter?"

"Well, I'm tired, for one thing. Workin' all day at the sawmill, tryin' to keep up with the chores on the farm, tinkerin' on broken tractors to make a little money on the side."

"And I hear you and Louis tryin' to build you a house."

"Yes'm, we are. Little by little," James sighed.

"Well, you boys can add a room to this house when you finish yours."

"We'll do it. Anything to please you, Miss Fannie."

"How Miss Betts?"

"I honestly don't know 'cause she don't have nothin' to do with me. She thinks I disgraced her when Sally Ann and I had to get married."

"You can't stop love. And babies is God's gift no matter when they show up. Miss Betts will come around."

"I'm not sure about that. I feel like an outcast in my own family the way I am treated. And Mama and Papa are supposed to be such good Christians. Well, where is the Christian charity when it comes to their own son?"

"Son, God works in mysterious ways. You got to keep the faith. The Bible says all things work together for good for them that love the Lord."

All this talk was making James feel more resentful than he already was. He knew Miss Fannie meant well, but he couldn't take any more of it.

"Well, it's good to see you, Miss Fannie. You keep Louis out of trouble. I better get home and see 'bout my wife."

Unconditional love is what he felt when he visited with Miss Fannie. He realized what a contrast this was to how he felt around his own mother.

Chapter 33

JAMES AND THE BABY

"How are you feeling, honey?" James asked as he finished washing up for Sunday supper.

"Well, my back hurts. My ankles are swollen. I'm running to the outhouse every few minutes. I feel like I'm carrying a watermelon around in front of me. But, other than that, I feel great." She laughed. "Really, thanks to you, James Dalton. I've never been happier."

What a wonderful wife I have, he thought. He was so tired; he bent to rest his head on the table while she finished getting supper on the table. The next thing he knew, he heard her voice coming from what seemed like a far away place. He roused at her touch and said, "Huh?" like someone who suddenly found himself in a strange place.

"Baby, you are working too much and too hard. I'm worried about you. You work seven days a week from early to late. Then, when you get home, you go outside to work on another project, like making our baby's crib. You don't get enough sleep. You will make yourself sick."

"I can do it. We need the money, and I want to get enough lumber to start our house. We are getting ahead, Sally Ann, little by little. I promise to be a good provider and give you what you deserve."

She looked so sweet. "I don't want all that much. I'd rather have more time with you. Why don't we ask Miss Betts to borrow her baby crib? She's not going to be using it anytime soon since there's no new baby on the way. And do you think you could maybe ask your Papa to give you a day off now and then?"

He didn't want to disappoint her. "I'll make us a crib. And I'll take some time off when the baby comes." *To hell with the work,* he thought. Papa would have to manage without him. He'd go to the sawmill, though; the pay was too good to give up.

James had invited Sally Ann's mother, Gertrude and sister, Bethany, to stay with them near the time the baby was expected. So Sally Ann would have someone there if he was at work when the baby arrived. Sally Ann had fixed them a pallet on the floor near the stove as their sleeping area. James overheard Gertrude talking to Sally Ann on the front porch.

"Baby, you ain't got nothing. Here you are about to have a baby. Why you living so poorly? I thought the Daltons had a-plenty. Why aren't y'all living in the big house?"

"We are fine. I love this cozy cabin, and besides, James has plans to build us a house. He plans to start next month. He wants us to be on our own to have our own family."

"Well, I hope that baby comes soon. My back hurts while sleeping on that hard floor. But I must admit, it is peaceful and quiet here, away from your daddy's raising hell all the time. Maybe I could live in this place when you and James get into your new house."

"Mama, are you okay? I worry Bethany is now getting treated like I was by Daddy. I feel guilty about leaving y'all."

"Don't worry about us. Johnny is getting big enough to handle ya daddy. We can stand it. He's drinking more than ever and passing out before he gets too mean."

Just then, a hard pain struck Sally Ann. She and Gertrude stared at each other, and they both knew the time had come.

James was mesmerized as he studied his newborn son. Wyatt had a mass of red hair, a deep shade of auburn. He was a good baby, and James doted on him. He hadn't yet wanted to take the baby up to meet his grandparents; too many of his siblings running around with colds was the excuse he gave Sally Ann. Papa had said he'd bring Mama down, but as the weeks passed, nobody came. James would be damned if he made the first move.

It was late one Sunday afternoon when James heard a "toot toot" of a car horn in the yard. He opened the door to see Martha in her new car. Martha leaned out the window and said, "Come on, you two; bring the baby and we'll take a ride in the country, go up to Batesville and get an ice cream cone."

Sally Ann was only too glad to get out of the house. However, James declined, saying he was working on a project. He knew Sally Ann got lonely now that her mama had returned home. She bundled up Wyatt in a hand-me-down blanket Martha had brought for the baby. James saw she felt adventurous as he waved them off.

Later, James wasn't surprised when Sally Ann told him what had happened.

"Might as well stop at the house to see if any of my little sisters want an ice cream cone," Martha had said as she pulled into the farmyard. Abigail and Tabitha were in the yard and raced to the car when Martha said, "Anyone want a ride and an ice cream cone?"

Sally Ann laughed when she told him that before Martha let the girls in the car, she said, "You have to go ask Mama." So both girls made a speedy U-turn back to the house. Soon Mama had appeared on the back porch.

James saw the kindness in Sally Ann's eyes as she told him that Martha had yelled to Mama to come see her beautiful red-headed grandson. She described how Mama had hesitated, looking out the screen door. Still, her curiosity got the better of her, and she headed down the back steps.

He saw the hint of tears as his wife described opening the car door so Mama could get a full view of the baby. Sally Ann explained how Mama had had eyes for no one but the baby as her face had softened, and a slow smile had crept across her face. Finally, Sally Ann told him the rest of what had happened. She had said, "Here, Miss Betts, you can hold him," as she lifted Wyatt up to his grandmother.

"Look, he just smiled at you, Mama. They say a baby this young can't recognize people, but he sure looked like he smiled at his grandmother," Martha said.

"Yes, he did," Mama had reportedly said.

James felt an inner glow of smug satisfaction because he wanted her to realize what she had been missing. But, at the same time, he hoped his mother had experienced the beginning of a bonding between herself and her new grandson and a thawing of her resentment of Sally Ann and disappointment with him.

Chapter 34

LYDIA NEEDS A PLAN

L ydia heard Martha's voice in the front room and hoped to have some private time with her. She heard small talk with Mama, and then the door opened slowly. Martha peered in as if she was afraid Lydia might be sleeping.

"Oh, do come in. I am so glad to see you." Lydia was more enthusiastic than usual. "I've been wanting to talk to you, Martha. See if you can help me persuade Mama about an idea I have."

Martha pulled up a chair and sat next to the bed. "I hope you are getting up and being more active. You'll never get your strength back if you don't push yourself a little." Martha was always the older sister giving advice, thought Lydia.

"Don't forget, I studied nursing and know the balance of rest and activity needed to recover from major surgery," Lydia responded with pride.

"The sooner you get well, the sooner you can return to nursing school."

"I'm done with nursing school. The work is too hard. I have to protect the one kidney I have left. What I really need is a different environment. I'm tired of this miserable scenery."

She sensed Martha's scorn. "Lydia! Don't be so ungrateful. You have a nice bedroom all to yourself, and you can see the weeping willow dancing in the wind outside your window. You have your younger sisters waiting on you hand and foot! And anyway, where do you think you'd have a better place to get well?"

"As a matter of fact, I know where."

Martha was clearly stunned and stayed quiet, waiting for Lydia to explain.

"Walter has invited me to come to Florida to recuperate. Sit in the sun and sip iced tea." Lydia gloated.

Martha sighed and took a breath. "I like Walter; he seems devoted to you. But you know as well as I that Mama would never stand for an unmarried daughter of hers going on any unescorted trip. I suppose you could get Abigail to go with you. But, even so, I don't think Mama would approve. So you better think of sitting right here in the Georgia sun."

Lydia scoffed at Martha's advice as her sister got up to go back in the kitchen when she heard Papa come in. Lydia watched the weeping willow tree swaying in the breeze as a plan began to form in her mind. She needed to stop everyone's pressuring her to go back to nursing school.

Chapter 35

LYDIA PROPOSES

Lydia wasn't surprised when Walter stopped by the house right on schedule the following week. She heard Mama open the door and ask him to wait in the parlor as she called Lydia. Lydia waited a few minutes before making her entrance. Thankfully, Mama had not stayed because she was busy canning tomatoes.

Walter always brought Lydia something; this time, she saw it was a beautiful tortoiseshell comb for her hair. She gracefully took her bobby pins out and let her hair fall down. Then, holding Walter's eye, she shook it out, stroked it, twisted it into a top knot, and inserted her new comb. The act was highly seductive, and Lydia could see its effect on Walter.

"How do I look?"

"Like the Queen of England!" His eyes were glistening, and his speech was breathy.

She held out her hand to him and said, "Then come hither and kiss my ring." When he came nearer, she put both hands on his face and kissed him straight on the lips. Then, before he could recover from his shock, she said, "I know what we should do! Let's ride down to my brother's place, where you can see the new baby."

"What a great idea. I'd love to!" Walter said.

She smiled as she sensed his delighted surprise. He was probably thinking how lucky he was.

Lydia got her sweater and started toward the front door. "Mama, we are heading down to James and Sally Ann's house. Be back in a few minutes." Mama appeared just as they were closing the door. *Too late to stop me*, thought Lydia.

Lydia knew they would be welcomed by Sally Ann, who loved to show off her new baby boy with his full head of auburn hair. She was a good mother and an excellent wife to James. Lydia liked Sally Ann, but thought she was too softhearted.

"What a nice surprise! Come in, Lydia and Walter," Sally Ann said.

Both James and Sally Ann had met Walter before and liked him. They didn't see a problem with the age difference, especially as James had said, because Lydia had always been an old soul.

They had a pleasant visit, and as they left, Lydia said to Walter, "Let's take a detour before we head back to my house. I love riding in your car. We can go down Thrill Hill and loop back to the main road."

Walter smiled with pleasure, and she saw he was grateful for the extra private time with her.

"I'd love to keep on riding. All the way to Florida," she said coquettishly and laid her head back against the seat. The movement caused her blouse to open slightly at the neck, revealing more of her lily-white chest.

Walter laughed delightedly, "Well, you have a standing invitation."

"Pull over at the church cemetery, and let's talk."

"The cemetery?" Walter looked concerned. She nodded.

"No one will bother us. They will think we're grieving and leave us alone," she grinned.

Lydia looked at Walter with a serious expression. "Walter, there is only one way I could go to Florida." She slid over and sat right next to him. Their eyes locked, and he, too, became serious.

He seemed clueless but stammered, "I'd be happy to have your mother or any of your sisters go too."

"No, that won't happen. There is only one way I can ever go to Florida, and that is as your wife."

Walter stared at her and had to make an effort to keep his mouth closed. She could see his thought process going from "impossible" to "maybe it's possible" to "what a good idea!"

"I would love for you to be my wife. I never dreamed you would want that too. What about your nursing? What about your family?"

"My nursing career is over. With only one kidney, I can never hope to finish school or work as a nurse. My family is my family whether I'm in Georgia or Florida."

"Well, okay, then. Let's get married. I will speak to your father as soon as we get back." Walter was gleeful now.

"No, there is no need to ask my father. It's a long story, but when Papa asked Mama's daddy for her hand, he got rejected, and there was a big falling out. Papa has always said his daughters may choose the man they love and his permission isn't necessary."

Lydia knew Walter was about to suggest they return and tell everyone at home.

"Walter, what I'd really like to do is elope. Otherwise, Mama will say I'm not well enough, and she will want to plan a wedding sometime in the future. But I don't want to wait. So what we will do is, the next time you come through, I'll have my suitcase ready, and we will slip out and leave a note.

"But I don't want to be sneaky."

"Don't worry, I will tell Papa, and if he is okay with it, he will make it all right with Mama."

"Okay, if you are sure. I don't want to get off on the wrong foot with your family."

"Trust me. This is the best way."

Lydia had convinced Walter to do as she wanted regarding her family. So, naturally, he was eager to tell his mother, knowing she would be delighted. And to blot out any other worries, Lydia gave him a long kiss.

Everything was going just as Lydia planned. Walter was coming back from Atlanta and headed for Florida in two weeks, and she had time to set the plan in motion. She told Mama she planned to spend some time at Martha's helping them get the store up and running, and she started packing her suitcase.

Mama had warned her to take it easy, and Lydia had assured her she would be working on setting up the books, not stocking the shelves. Thankfully, Mama didn't suspect anything and didn't check with Martha.

Even though Mama and Papa both liked Walter as a friend who shared the love of books, Lydia knew they would balk at her marrying him and moving to Florida. Mama wanted her to go back to nursing school and marry someone local because she wanted all her brood under her nose forever. Or if Lydia never married, she could stay home and see her parents through their old age—a job that Lydia did not want.

Sometimes, Lydia couldn't believe she was actually going to do it and even wavered occasionally.

Nevertheless, she packed her suitcase and anxiously awaited the day Walter would come by. It was a Sunday morning when she had told him to arrive. The time when everyone would be at church.

If I do this, there will be no turning back. I have tried to leave home before, only to have fate thrust me right back here on this farm. So if I am ever going to do it, now is the time.

She took a deep breath and opened the door. The suitcase was packed and ready. Was she really going to elope and run off to Florida? To spend the rest of her life with Walter? Mama would be furious. All the family would think she had lost her mind.

Lydia didn't care. Life had not been fair to her. A chance of happiness for an invalid like her didn't come along every day.

Chapter 36

LYDIA'S NEW LIFE

During the ride to Florida, Walter began telling Lydia more details about his home.

"I don't remember if I told you that my mother is nearly blind, Lydia. She manages very well, but it does mean that we have to keep everything in its place. At mealtime, I tell her what is on her plate and where it is located, which is all the help she needs to eat. Twelve o'clock is the peas, etc. When I am gone, my cousin, Annie, comes in to see about her meals and to check on her. And our maid, Lula Mae, comes to clean every day and help Mother with her bath. Lula Mae also prepares the evening meal and leaves it on the stove before she goes home." Walter wanted to be sure Lydia would be prepared to make her new home in Florida.

Lydia did not intend to take on any responsibilities for his mother. It sounded like he had it already worked out, and her care was handled by others. However, she was glad the maid would be cooking and cleaning. She planned to spend her afternoons reading and resting on the veranda.

"Lydia, you have always been an adventure seeker. I don't want you to get bored in the house all day. You are still recuperating but too young to be idle."

"Well, aren't you the sweetest thing to worry about my adventurous spirit? My dear Walter, I will be perfectly content to get my adventures in books and conserve my energy. I am content with a life of the mind. With only one kidney, I can't exert myself."

"I see you brought a book along. What are you reading?"

"I'm reading *Walden Pond* by Henry David Thoreau."

"Never heard of him."

Lydia turned her head away from him as she raised her eyebrows.

She wasn't sure what Walter would think if there were a silent gap in the conversation, so she kept talking. "Your mother must be so brave. How does Miss Jenny spend her day? Does she have someone to read to her?"

"Oh, she has Braille books and does very well entertaining herself. I'm sure she will enjoy your company, though."

Walter went on to tell her that his mother was thrilled when he told her he would be bringing his new bride home. Lydia thought to herself, *I must establish from the beginning that I am the lady of the household but that I am an invalid and need constant rest.*

Lydia confirmed that Miss Jenny was as self-sufficient as Walter had described. Between Annie and Lula Mae, Lydia had an easy life. As the months went on, Lydia was content with Walter, and he said he had never been happier in his whole life. He called her his delicate sweetheart and vowed he would do anything to take care of her and see that she had no regrets. Walter continued to bring her surprise gifts, anything to delight her. He had canceled two trips to Atlanta, so he could get her settled and his mother comfortable with the transition in the household.

When Walter wasn't traveling to Atlanta, he went into the office by eight every morning and was home shortly after five. Lydia spent her day reading and napping. She had plenty of time to write in her journal about how life in Florida was so different from life on the farm.

Lula Mae's cooking had to be modified as she was used to frying the meat in leftover bacon grease and overcooking the vegetables. Lydia taught her what she had learned in nursing school about healthy eating—how to broil meat instead of frying—and cook vegetables without fat.

Nevertheless, Lula Mae made biscuits every day, which they all loved. She always left a pie or cake of some sort, as Miss Jenny had a sweet tooth. To do her domestic duty, Lydia put their dishes in the sink for Lula Mae to take care of the following day. She, Walter, and Miss Jenny then spent the evening hearing about Walter's job, discussing the local news, and listening to mystery programs on the radio.

It wasn't long before the sisters started coming for a visit. It was an adventure for them, the first time they had ever gone past the county line, much less left the state. Tabitha had met Leland, a younger friend of Walter's, so she came to visit more and more often. Lydia was always glad for the company and liked showing how Walter pampered her. She always made it clear that company would have to fend for themselves.

Chapter 37

MARTHA'S NEWS

It happened two months after the store opened. Was it the smell of the bologna in the meat display case? Whatever it was, Martha threw up her breakfast and had to lie down in the store's back room.

The store was doing well. It was a large room in which Martha and Elbert had organized the displays of bread, canned goods, fresh vegetables and fruit, and dairy products. There was a large meat case with scales and plenty of butcher paper and staple goods on shelves against the wall. Candy and gum were displayed near the cash register. Soft drinks were in the big Coca-Cola case on the porch—an easier place to drain the melted ice each night. Many neighborhood patrons stopped by the store on their way home from work.

The second time nausea hit her, Martha became worried. "Oh, no, no, no. Please, no." By the third time, she knew it was so. She put off telling anyone, hoping she could ignore it a little longer. But of course she could count, and she knew the possibilities. She did her own problem-solving and decided she would have to face it. She hoped and prayed that maybe this child would look like her side of the family. When she was about four months along, she told Elbert she was expecting.

"That is wonderful news! I'm going to be a father again! Maybe it will be a boy this time. Should we name him 'Junior?' Mattie will love a little brother."

Martha almost choked. "Well, it may be a girl, you know. We will have to wait and see." She busied herself rearranging the bread display.

"You don't seem very pleased or excited, Martha. Is something wrong?"

"Nothing wrong. Just the timing. I wish we had the store better established, that's all."

"The store is doing fine. We will be fine. We have the room in the back here; you can lie down and rest whenever you want. I can't wait to share the news with Mother and Frederick. Frederick will be so jealous that I am getting ahead of him!"

They had decided that when the baby dropped, Martha would go to her mother's place and await the birth. Mama was an experienced midwife, and there were plenty of sisters to help. It was women's work, after all. Mattie would go with her, and she was looking forward to being with the big family. Even though the two girls were the same age, Miriam as Martha's youngest sister was Mattie's aunt. They giggled when Mattie would tease her by calling her "Aunt Miriam." Because Miriam's two younger brothers couldn't say her name, she had become "Mot." Elbert would see to the store but come out to the farm every night to check on Martha.

When Martha's labor started early one morning, things moved slowly. The pains grew worse, and Martha was covered in sweat as each new contraction left her exhausted. Betts determined the baby was breech and knew it would be a long and challenging process. As the young ones were eating breakfast, the pain became unbearable, and Martha let out a loud cry.

"What's the matter with Mommy?" Mattie sounded alarmed.

"She's all right. Abigail, you take Mattie and Miriam outside to play. Keep them out there until I call you to come in. Hurry now," Betts said.

It was a cold and windy day. Mattie did not have a coat, but Abigail gave her an old blanket to put around her shoulders. The children went to the playhouse made from tree branches and made mud pies all morning. Then, Abigail went back to the house to help Mama.

In the warmth of the house, between contractions, Martha couldn't help thinking about that brutal night at Sam's home. This delivery was not unlike that kind of agony. She just wanted it to be over.

Abigail wiped her sweating face with a cold rag, and it felt so good. By noon, there was not much progress, and Mama had had no success trying to turn the baby. Mama believed in patience and prayer, and she didn't want to call the doctor unless it was absolutely necessary.

Since Martha's cries had gotten too loud to disguise and Mama had instructed the little girls to stay outside, Phoebe fixed peanut butter sandwiches and told them they could have a picnic in the barn but to be careful not to disturb the horses. They wanted to stay in their playhouse, but Phoebe insisted they go to the pump to wash their hands before going to the barn.

Chapter 38

MARTHA'S LONG LABOR AND LOSS

"Brr, this water is ice cold," said Mattie as she held her hands under the spout while Miriam pumped. The water splashed down the front of her dress.

"I want to come inside. I'm cold, Aunt Phoebe," Mattie said.

"I'm cold too," said Miriam.

Phoebe saw their lips had a bluish tinge, and their hands were cold as ice.

"If you are cold, go to the barn; it's warmer there. You'll have a new baby brother or sister soon. Then you can come in."

"I want a sister, and tell her to hurry up."

It was late afternoon when the baby boy finally arrived. Martha was exhausted, but she anxiously examined the baby.

"Looking to see if he has all his toes?" Abigail said.

"What? Oh yes." The baby had dark hair, very different from Mattie's hair color. His eyes were blue for now, but Mama had said all babies have blue eyes at first. His facial features weren't distinct. He just looked like any baby. Martha sighed and handed him back to Mama to clean up.

Martha knew that Elbert was overjoyed to have a son. They had decided against "Junior" and instead to name him after Elbert's grandfather, Mason Chesterfield. Elbert bought a supply of cigars with blue wrappers to give his customers. Martha was to stay at her mother's home for the rest of the week to regain her strength.

By mid-morning the next day, Mattie was sniffling and not feeling well. Martha heard Mama tell Elbert to take her down to James and Sally Ann's place so she wouldn't expose the baby if she were coming down with something. Little Wyatt was eighteen months old now, a sturdy boy and walking around all over the cabin. If Mattie didn't recover by the end of the day, Elbert would come and get her and take her back to town with him. Martha knew that Sally Ann would be glad to help and would welcome Mattie, who was still complaining of being cold.

Later Martha learned that Sally Ann had fixed her a cup of hot cocoa, and Mattie had enjoyed watching Wyatt, who was full of energy. Elbert told her that when Mattie felt hot to the touch in the afternoon, she fell asleep on the couch. Sally Ann had said their phone was out of order and she couldn't call Elbert about her concern, but she had to wait until he closed the store and made the trip to the farm. Elbert said when he saw how sick Mattie was, he wrapped her up in a quilt and put her in the car.

"I decided to go by and pick up Mother and take her home with me to take care of Mattie," Elbert said.

Martha overheard that Miriam had also developed a cough and a fever, and Mama was doctoring her at home. Martha was worried about Mattie but knew Elbert and Miss Lucille would take good care of her. Elbert told her that Mattie had developed a deep cough and runny nose the next day. He had called the doctor to make a house call.

After listening to Mattie's chest, the doctor declared she had croup. He prescribed sulfa medication and instructed Miss Lucille about bathing her with cool water to reduce the fever. Unfortunately, Mattie didn't seem to respond to these treatments, and two days later, the doctor was back. Martha was more and more worried.

Elbert told Martha, "I'm afraid its bad news. It has settled in her lungs and has turned into pneumonia. The doctor said to keep a steamer going in the room so she can breathe better. She needs lots of rest, and we must make her drink water. We'll have to wait it out. Watch and pray." Miriam seemed to get better, and they hoped Mattie would too.

Elbert was really worried. He had been giving Martha daily reports. She wanted to come home, but Elbert and Mama were adamantly opposed. She was torn between her newborn's and her daughter's needs. In the end, she couldn't control the situation. Martha had no way to get back to town, even if she had defied their advice.

As Elbert explained to Martha, his mother kept vigil during the day and slept upstairs at night. His schedule was to open up the store each morning, go home for lunch, check on Mattie, close up the store at the end of the day, and make a quick visit to the farm to check on Martha and their baby son. Then, he would return home and sit by Mattie's bed all night.

Elbert would doze off sitting in the chair but wake whenever Mattie had a coughing spell. He told Martha that the doctor came twice a day now but could see no improvement. Finally, five days after Elbert had brought her home Mattie became unconscious.

Martha insisted on going home; Miss Lucille could take care of baby Mason. She knelt by Mattie's bedside and prayed and talked to Mattie just before that pale, listless child took her last breath.

"Oh, God, no!" Martha wailed.

Chapter 39

MARTHA'S AGONY

Martha went into a deep depression. She felt guilty. It was her fault. She considered all of the "what-ifs." If she hadn't gotten pregnant. If she could have delivered the baby quickly instead of taking all day with Mattie out in the cold. If she could have muffled her cries so Mattie could have stayed inside.

She felt sorry for Mason not ever knowing his loving sister. She burst into tears at the thought of Mattie not getting to hold her little brother. They tried to tell her it was God's will, but that made her mad. They said Mattie was in a better place, but that didn't stop the ache of wanting her here. Her milk dried up as the tears poured. Mason had to be fed with a bottle. She held him, but she was so sorrowful that he seemed to feel her tension.

Martha and the baby were brought home, and Mama came too, as much to tend to her as the baby. Gradually Martha began to pick up the pieces and realized life must go on. But she was only going through the motions.

She could not bear to look at Sam's Department Store whenever they drove past. She hated Sam even more. He was such an evil man. She saw the connections between all the events following his assault on her. She hadn't shared this with anyone but Sally Ann and holding this anger inside was tearing her to pieces.

Not even her revenge made the pain go away. Elbert was tender with her, but she could tell he was getting tired of living in such a melancholy atmosphere. He had long days in the store and didn't need to come home to more problems.

Martha could see this but didn't have the energy to do anything about it. Mama's sister, Aunt Dolly, had volunteered to stay with the children at the farm while Mama came to take care of Martha. Mama had been there three weeks, reading the Bible to her, but without any reaction from Martha. Then one day, her mother announced she was going home at the end of the week. Martha knew that Mama hoped this would jolt her out of her black mood.

It had been two years since Mattie died; Mason was thriving and into everything. Martha felt she was functioning well, but Elbert could tell the sadness was still at the bottom of her heart. She had no joy in life and was just putting one foot in front of the other. She tried to hide how much she dwelled on thoughts of Mattie, but she knew Elbert could sense it.

She recognized Elbert's kindness. "Let's go to the picture show this weekend. I can go get Phoebe to visit, and she can babysit Mason. She will love that. Maybe cheer you up too. She always has lively stories about what she's been up to."

"Okay, if you like," Martha smiled and tried to show a little enthusiasm.

They parked in front of the movie theater, and since they had arrived before the show started, they decided to walk around the block and look in the shop windows. Martha had always liked merchandising and display windows, and the stroll indeed seemed to wake up some interest in her.

When they returned to the show, Elbert pointed out an empty store nearby. It had been an antique shop; apparently, people weren't that interested and probably had enough old things at home. The building was narrow and seemed to be extended to match the length of the movie theater.

Elbert said, "Hmmm. I wonder what kind of store will be going in here? It will be ideal for someone. Everyone who goes to the movie will have to pass right by."

The show was a musical with Carmen Miranda. It was very lively, and it did indeed perk Martha up. She felt she could move on for the first time and leave the sadness tucked away in the back corner of her heart. But it wasn't really the movie that perked Martha up. Instead, that empty store had awakened a long-ago dream.

A week after Martha opened her boutique, La Couture, right next to the downtown movie theater, she found out she was pregnant.

Elbert laughed, "Every time we open a store, you get pregnant!"

Chapter 40

ABIGAIL MEETS THE DUNAWAYS

Abigail put on a bravado attitude about her nervousness while getting ready to meet Doug's entire family at Sunday dinner.

"I can't wear this blue dress; it looks faded!" she wailed.

Mama admonished her as she pulled the hem down as far as it would go. "It does not; it's meant to be light blue. And it looks great with your strawberry blonde hair."

"You mean this mop that just won't curl?"

"Stop criticizing what the Lord gave you. Pretty is as pretty does." She had heard these words from Mama a thousand times.

With the devil in her eyes, little sister Phoebe said, "If they have fried chicken, don't pick it up with your fingers."

"Abigail knows her manners," said Miriam, ever the peacemaker.

"Remember when you spilled your tea all over the tablecloth when the preacher was here?" Abigail knew Phoebe couldn't help goading her older sister.

"Oh, stop it, Phoebe. I won't tell you a thing about what happens if you keep up that kind of talk." Phoebe pursed her lips together but couldn't hide the mischievous smile.

"Just remember, Doug is sweet on you, and you have nothing to worry about." Mama and all the girls had gathered around to watch Abigail get dressed. They shared in the excitement of this significant event, which might lead to an engagement. Just then, the doorbell clanged. Phoebe and Miriam ran to get it, with Abigail telling them to stop. She didn't want the whole family to act like they couldn't wait for Doug to get there.

Abigail liked that Doug was quiet and calm and depended on her to carry the conversation. All he did was smile at her with his big blue eyes and puppy dog grin. Their relationship had developed over the past year when her father had introduced them. Doug drove the big truck that delivered the gas to their country store.

"A good steady job," Papa had said, "and one likely to have opportunities in the future." She suspected he didn't express his main thought: that Abigail had a little wild streak and a headstrong nature. Doug's mild personality was just the kind of match she needed.

Doug helped her into the car, and they rode without saying a word. She knew Doug probably sensed her nervousness, and he didn't want to disrupt her with needless talk. It was a short ride to the Dunaway farm but seemed interminable with dead silence.

She took a deep breath as they arrived and walked across the wide front porch. She was introduced to all of Doug's family as they sat around the parlor, waiting for the ham to finish roasting. Polite, get-to-know-you conversation. Abigail could smell the food, and judging by the plumpness of all the family members, she knew the meal would be delicious.

When everyone was seated around the big table, Doug's father said a fervent prayer, blessing the food and thanking God for bringing this visitor to their home and family. Abigail felt confident among the relatives and said "Amen" along with the others. As the steaming hot dishes were being passed around, there was a loud bang, like the front door slamming extra hard. Abigail was as shocked as everyone.

Doug's mother jumped and said, "Good Lord, what was that?" Just then, a tall, gangly man wearing blue jeans, a western-cut plaid shirt, and a cowboy hat entered the dining room.

"What? Having dinner without me? What the hell is going on?"

Abigail was fascinated. She stared, as did everyone else.

"Dirk," Mrs. Dunaway rose from the table, "Goodness, you gave us a scare. And watch your language. How could we have known you would be coming home? Where on earth have you been this time? Here, sit down. I'll get you a plate." She reached behind her in the hutch for a plate and silverware.

"I've been on a cattle drive out in Texas. Fending off the cattle rustlers and watching out for Injuns."

"Well, Mr. Texas, take your hat off when you sit at my table." Everyone started passing the dishes as Mrs. Dunaway went to the kitchen for a glass of iced tea.

Abigail could hardly take her eyes off this handsome fellow, with some resemblance to Doug; the same features but arranged just differently enough to give him a dashing look. She noticed the scowl on Mr. Dunaway's face as he said, "Your timing is impeccable, as always, Dirk. If you know so much about cattle, maybe you can help us around here." Doug said not a word, just picked up his fork and ate with gusto.

Abigail felt herself blush—darn her Irish complexion—when Dirk winked at her and said, "Isn't anyone going to introduce me to this beautiful gal who is gracing our dinner table?"

Mrs. Dunaway quickly responded, "This is Abigail Dalton, and she is Doug's guest. Her folks live over in

Beulah; you would have met them if you ever went to church there."

"Yum. Yum. Best ham I've had in months. A lot better than eating rabbit cooked over a campfire." Dirk continued to dominate the conversation for the rest of the meal as Doug and his father sat silently, withdrawing from the conversation. Abigail forgot Phoebe's warning about spilling her tea, mesmerized by this larger-than-life character who seemed to thoroughly enjoy himself, not seeming to care that others obviously disapproved of him. Abigail had the strangest feeling—something had changed.

Chapter 41

ABIGAIL AND DIRK

Abigail heard the knock on the door as she finished dressing. "Doug is early!" She heard Mama call her to announce Mr. Dunaway. They were going to the picture show in town, a special treat.

She picked up her pocketbook and sweater and headed for the door, calling "goodbye" to her sisters. The smile froze on her face, and her pace slowed as she saw it was not Doug but Dirk who had been shown into the parlor. My, but he was dashingly handsome.

"Doug sent me to get you. He had to finish up at work and didn't want y'all to be late for the movie." She hesitated and knitted her brows together. Then, as if sensing she would need more convincing, he continued.

"Something came up last minute, and you know how particular Doug is about taking care of his customers." That eased her mind, but she was still skeptical. He made a move to leave, and she had no choice but to follow as he took her elbow and guided her out the door. She felt a little thrill as he helped her into his car.

"The three of us going to the movie? A strange sort of date."

Dirk flashed her one of his crooked smiles and said, "Well, Abby, maybe we should skip the movie and run away together." He drove faster than she was used to.

"You look extra special tonight, Abby." She laughed at his silliness, but her laugh faded as he turned off the main highway toward the old church cemetery.

"Why are we going this way?" She quickly saw a misadventure coming.

"Don't you know? This is a shortcut to the movie."

"Now, listen here. I have lived in this town my whole life, and this is no shortcut to anywhere. So what are you doing?"

"Just taking a little detour, sugar babe. We have time to spare."

She had to admit she felt that thrill again. Doug never called her sweet names. He was so predictable; she had not realized how good it felt to hear endearments and to have a little mystery and surprise in one's life.

"I wanted you to see this picturesque view. Someday, I will own this land and build a sprawling plantation right here. Wouldn't you like to live in a place like that?"

Could she picture herself there? With Dirk? She felt the mysterious pull of such a vision. But she had a practical side to her nature, too. She wasn't sure he could settle down and have any kind of stable life.

"I thought you liked to roam around and experience life. I can't see you settled down, working a farm."

"I could, with the right woman at my side." She jerked around, and he met her eyes and held them. Her heart fluttered, and she took a deep breath.

"We'd better head back to that movie. Doug will beat us there," he said as if trying to lighten the mood.

And sure enough, when the car pulled up to the movie theater, Doug was there, looking mildly annoyed, which was about as upset as Doug ever got. He walked over to the car window on Dirk's side.

"You lousy scoundrel. When I got to Abigail's house, they said you had just picked her up."

Dirk gave a roaring laugh and replied, "Just playing a joke on you, little brother. Y'all enjoy the movie."

She saw the annoyed expression on Doug's face. A misadventure indeed! Where would this all end?

Chapter 42

ABIGAIL AND THE BOX SUPPER

A bigail helped Miriam tie the ribbon on her box for the church supper. "It's time to go," Papa called out.

It was the big night of the box supper at Beulah Community Center. The annual fundraiser this time was for new church choir robes. The eligible girls packed supper for two in a box, and the eligible men in the community bid on them, getting both the supper and the girl to go with it. The men weren't supposed to know whose box was whose, but somehow most of them figured it out. Abigail, Phoebe and Miriam had packed their boxes with fried chicken, deviled eggs, pimento cheese sandwiches, Mama's homemade pickles, and slabs of pound cake—more than enough for two. They had wrapped the boxes in red paper but tied each with a different color ribbon for identification.

Known as Beulah, the center of the community was about five miles from home. The drive was a pleasant one with fields of corn, peanuts and cotton on either side of the road. Cattle grazed in pastures of neighboring farms. The church was the little white clapboard sanctuary connected to an annex of rooms on each side of a hall. The rooms were for the Sunday School classes—one each for toddlers, young children and youth—and separate rooms for women's and men's classes.

There was also a nursery where the babies were tended by church volunteers so the parents could attend the services. Across from the church was the larger building, the schoolhouse. It was made of brick, a rectangular building, more functional than attractive. The front entrance was straight up the stairs and then into the hall, with classrooms to the left and right and a large auditorium in the center.

The auditorium was where the box supper auction would take place. Between the church and the school several oak trees shaded picnic tables where "dinner on the grounds" was held once a month. Behind the church was the Beulah cemetery. Just about every church member had generations of relatives resting in peace there.

When they arrived at the school, most of the young men were milling around outside, intent on catching a glance of the box their sweetheart carried in. Abigail saw that Doug was among the men, and he and Abigail gave each other a conspiratorial grin. There was much flurry as about twenty girls brought their boxes to the front of the auditorium. The stage was bare, but the brightly colored packages and ribbons lent a festive atmosphere. When all the boxes were assembled, the church music director, acting as auctioneer, offered a prayer and then the bidding began.

"This first box here smells mighty good, and it's heavy too! Now, who will give me $1 for this box?" the auctioneer hawked.

It sold to Joe Fortner for $3, and Miss Alice Burrows acknowledged it was hers. The two left for a picnic table outside. Jimmy Johnson and Bob Ferris bid on the next box until it reached $4.50, and Bob gave a shout. The lively Miss Bunny Burrows joined the winner, and no one was surprised that this duo ended up together. Frederick Hall bid on and won Rachel's box.

"Next up is this pretty red box, tied with a white ribbon, and I know it's full of goodies," said the auctioneer. Doug, recognizing the box, bid $2 right off the bat. From the back of the room came "$10!" There was a gasp as Dirk stepped out and walked forward.

Then there was silence until the barker said, "Sold to Dirk Dunaway for $10!"

Abigail was as shocked as everyone else, but she saw that Doug was crestfallen. Standing beside Doug, she heard his mother say, "Isn't it nice your brother wants to help the church? And now he will also get to know his future sister-in-law."

Trying to keep his face a mask, Doug responded meekly, "Yes, I'm sure he will."

Abigail was thrilled but concerned about what others would think. Dirk paid up the $10 and came over to where Abigail was standing with Doug, saying, "I've been eager to try Miss Betts' cooking. Come on, Abby."

Outside they saw the others who had paired off at the picnic tables around the church and schoolyard. One couple had settled on the ground, apart from everyone. Abigail had gotten her sweater, preparing to join the others outside.

But Dirk guided her into the church annex and toward a small room, the room where the children attended Sunday School. All the tables and chairs were small for the little children. There were sheets of drawing paper lining the walls with children's handprints in red with the greeting, "Happy Mother's Day." Color crayons were neatly stacked in bins, and various toys of all shapes and sizes were on the shelves.

"Let's sit on the floor, Abby. We can be private in here, and I've been wanting to talk to you." Abigail felt a little uneasy over this choice and started over to turn on the light switch. "No, no," Dirk said. "Let's eat with just the moonlight."

It was growing dusk, and the room had the aura of candlelight. Abigail was very nervous, like they were doing something they shouldn't. But Dirk was such a strong personality, she took the easy way out and acquiesced. They opened the box and started eating. Dirk oohed and aahed with the first bite of each item.

"You wanted to talk to me?" Abigail said.

"Yes, tell me all about yourself," said Dirk. "What you like, what you hate, what you want out of life, why you would settle for that pipsqueak little brother of mine."

"Well, I come from a big family, mostly girls. I live on a farm. I go to school. I go to church. That's about it."

"Naw, that's not who you are. What do you want? What makes you so mad you could spit? What makes you happy?"

"I never thought about those things. Well, let's see... I want a husband and children eventually, a nice home."

"That's so ordinary! What about travel? Adventure? Wild parties?"

"That sounds okay. Yes, that would make me happy." She was still shy and could tell he was trying to pull something out of her.

"What would you do today if you knew it was your last day on earth?" he said.

She immediately thought *I'd kiss you,* but she kept silent.

"I know what I'd do," he said. He leaned toward her and held her eyes. The light was fading with only a trace of moonlight shining through one of the windows.

"What makes me mad is when my sisters tell me what to do like I don't have a lick of sense." Abigail quickly filled in the growing silence.

"Aha. You are a woman of independent spirit. I like that."

"The happiest I remember being is my first time at the picture show. I felt like I was in a different world for a while."

"See, you do like adventure. I have to have adventure, or else I will go crazy. I don't like to conform to what others think I should do. I have a different opinion about how life should be lived than my family does. I think you are the same but afraid to step out on your own path. You need someone like me to encourage you."

Again, he held her eyes, and she became uncomfortable. "We'd better go back and join the others," she said. His talk of family had reminded her that hers would be wondering where they had disappeared to.

After packing up the remains, Dirk moved over to one of the chairs obviously meant for the teacher. He gently pulled Abigail into his lap. She was immediately frantic, thinking *If someone came by, entered the room, and turned on the light....*

But somehow, the audacity of what they were doing gave her a thrill like nothing she had ever experienced. He pulled her to him and kissed her full on the lips. She resisted only a few seconds, then melted into his arms and kissed him back. It was pure bliss.

Abigail and Dirk came out of the annex just as the others from the grounds went back into the church, and they blended in with the crowd. Doug apparently had ended up with Abigail's youngest sister's box, and Miriam was thrilled to have spent some time with Abigail's beau. Dirk leaned down to Abigail and said, "I've got to go. Don't answer any questions."

"Are you going home before the singing?" She was surprised but relieved.

"Number one: I can't sing, and number two: No, I'm not going home, as in my Mama and Daddy's, where the house rules are too strict for me. I'm staying with friends of mine in town, Mary Bell and Jake."

Abigail ended up sitting with some girls for the sing-fest. When Doug looked around, he saw her. She returned his smile and tried to look innocent though he was obviously wondering about Dirk. Of course if anyone asked, she would say he ate in a hurry and left, so she joined her girlfriends.

Chapter 43

ABIGAIL GOES TO VISIT

Abigail couldn't believe her good luck when Mama said to her the next week, "Martha needs help with the baby and with Mason. A two-year-old gets into everything, and Eliza still takes a bottle every four hours. Martha pushes herself too hard, running a dress shop with two little babies and only Flossie to help. And Elbert is certainly no help at home."

Mama had a furrowed look on her face as she sat crocheting. "Abigail, I think you should go and stay with them for the next two weeks until Flossie feels comfortable handling the children and the housework while Martha is at the store."

Abigail was glad enough to go spend some time in town. She didn't mind babies; goodness knows she had sufficient training from her own little brothers and sisters. And besides, Jake and Mary Bell lived about two blocks from Martha and Elbert's house.

Martha's house was right across from the high school ball field, and Abigail loved visiting it. The house was a two-story white wooden house with green shutters. It had a wide front porch with rocking chairs and a front door painted black, of all things. As you entered, the living room was to the left and the dining room to the right. The brick fireplace on the east end had been painted white to match the walls, giving the place a look of sophistication. Martha had made the heavy drapes which added to the room's rich decor.

The oversized kitchen and back porch were behind the dining room on the right. Past the living room was a hallway with a small bathroom. On the other side of the stairs was a big bedroom. The stairs off the hallway led up to two additional bedrooms and a bath. The size of the house was perfect for a family to raise a girl and a boy, and it was close to the schools they would attend. Abigail was very comfortable in an upstairs bedroom across the hall from Mason. For now, the baby's crib was in Martha and Elbert's bedroom downstairs.

On the first day of her visit, Abigail stayed reasonably busy with the baby and Mason, who was a bundle of energy. Flossie was a natural with both children and had a pleasant temperament while she worked. When Martha returned from the store, Flossie had dinner on the stove, and the baby was sleeping. Mason, so glad to see his mother, flew into her arms.

"Why don't you get some fresh air, Abigail? I know you have been cooped up inside all day. The neighborhood is a nice, safe place to walk, and you might even see a practice ballgame going on." Abigail agreed it would be good to stretch her legs and be outside with nature. The dogwood trees were in full bloom this time of year. It was still a couple of hours before dark.

She didn't even try to squelch her excitement knowing she would head straight to Jake and Mary Bell's house, and hoping that Dirk would be there. She was too nervous to notice there was no car in the shed as she knocked on the door. Then, just as she was about to give up and leave, the door opened, and Dirk, with tousled hair and sleep in his eyes, opened the door.

"Oh, sorry. Did I wake you?" Abigail stammered, feeling that darn Irish blush again.

"I fell asleep on the couch—didn't get much sleep last night."

"I came by to see Mary Bell. I'm staying with my sister down the street."

"Well, come on in," Dirk ushered her in and shut the door. He yelled, "Mary Bell!" while Abigail stood confused in the silence. "Oh, I forgot, she and Jake had to go see about her daddy. I think he fell this afternoon. So they'll be gone another couple of hours at least."

Abigail felt a thrill being here with just the two of them but knew she shouldn't stay with him alone. She didn't trust the situation—whether him or herself, she couldn't say. "I'd better go then. I'll come back another time."

"Now, sugar babe, no need to rush off. I've been by myself all afternoon and could use a little company. You're a big girl who don't need to be chaperoned."

"Well, I can't stay but a minute, anyway. Martha will be getting supper together, and I should help." She remained standing to reinforce her declaration that she did not intend to stay long. Dirk moved closer to her, and her pulse raced. She tried backing up, but he took hold of her arm. "Did anyone ever tell you that you have the most beautiful... eyes... body?" She wouldn't move an inch lest he thought he was intimidating her.

"All the time. I get tired of hearing it. Can't you come up with something less corny?"

Dirk burst out laughing and bent backward with his hands on his hips.

"I like a sassy woman!" He moved toward her again, and she sidestepped around him. He took both her shoulders this time and said, "I'll let you go for just one kiss." She cocked her head and tried to assess him. Would he keep his word or just keep kissing her until she went mad? Either way, she knew she was doomed.

The next night when she came to the house, Jake and Mary Bell were there and were delighted to see her. The four of them sat in the backyard and enjoyed the evening breeze. The shade of their big magnolia tree was cool, and the blossoms' fragrance made Abigail want to sit there all night. She felt welcome, and her visits became a nightly event. Sometimes the four of them played cards; Dirk was quite good at whatever they played, and he and Abigail were natural partners.

"Abigail, you have to come to our party Saturday night. We are celebrating our fifth anniversary. As the song goes, 'we got married in a fever.' Jake was worried my daddy would disapprove, so we decided to elope. Went over to Putnam County to a Justice of the Peace."

"I think eloping is the best way to get married," said Dirk, looking straight at Abigail. "Avoid all the fuss and get right down to business," he said with a wicked grin.

"My sisters Lydia and Rachel both eloped," said Abigail, "and my parents were very upset."

"But they were just as married," Dirk said. Abigail liked that he was so independent and didn't care if anyone liked what he did or not. In her household, the appearance of something was more important than the actual facts.

Abigail wore her light blue dress to the party Saturday night. She remembered this was what she had worn the night she first met Dirk, which seemed so long ago, although it was only a few weeks. This made her think of Doug, poor Doug. She had been trying to decide how to tell him about her and Dirk. She knew he would be crushed, but it couldn't be helped. There were plenty of other girls who would appreciate him. After all, she and Doug weren't suited for each other—their personalities were too different. After he got over his hurt feelings, he would probably be happy for her and Dirk and realize they were a better match.

The party was well underway when Abigail arrived with a cherry pie she had made. She could tell Dirk was very impressed. He pretended to smell the pie, nudged up against her, and brushed against her breast. There were about five couples there, and the radio played some jazzy music. Two couples were dancing.

The drink station was laid out in a help-yourself fashion in the small kitchen. Dirk fixed a drink and said, "Kentucky's finest." Abigail had had very little liquor in her life, mostly in eggnog at Christmas. So she decided to act like she was used to it, just like Dirk was doing.

In the living room, Abigail noticed one of the couples was missing, and just as she was about to ask if they had already gone home, a bedroom door opened, and the couple emerged. Everyone else started oohing and aahing, and they both grinned.

Dirk, it turned out, was a superb dancer. She remembered how Doug danced with two left feet. The lights had been turned off, and the candles glowed softly, creating the perfect blend with the gentle breeze through the open windows for a dreamy atmosphere. Abigail felt happy, content, and excited all at once. When Dirk took her into the back bedroom, it felt like the most natural thing in the world.

The two weeks at Martha's were almost up, and Mama had sent word that she expected Abigail back home on Sunday. Elbert would drive them all there for Sunday dinner so the rest of the family could see the children. It had been the most glorious two weeks of Abigail's life, getting to see Dirk every day and watching their love blossom. She had given herself over to him several times; they were hungry for each other. He hadn't said anything about what they would do when she was no longer in town, but she suspected his mind was working on that obstacle.

He had not ever come to see Abigail at Martha's, which was understandable since Martha would have wondered about Doug. Martha only knew that Abigail went to visit Mary Bell and Jake, and she encouraged her to be with people her own age after a day of childcare. Dirk had walked her home the night of the party, and Abigail had hurried up the stairs before anyone could smell the alcohol on her breath.

She packed her things and decided she had to put on an act to be glad to see Mama and the little ones at home. Three days passed with no word from Dirk, and she began to stew. She kept telling herself he would likely pop up and surprise her like he had done several times before. Abigail had to curb her impatience, but where was he?

Several weeks passed with no word. Had he gone back to Texas? Maybe he was trying to earn more money so they could marry when he returned. On the other hand, he probably didn't know how to contact her while he was gone but knew she would be waiting for him. That had to be it.

Chapter 44

MARTHA'S BOUTIQUE

The boutique's success exceeded all expectations. Instead of competing with the well-established department stores in town that tried to meet everyone's needs, La Couture specialized in women's attire, stocking everything from basic foundations to outer garments, shoes, hats and gloves. It was a woman's paradise, with female clerks ready to assist and encourage shoppers to pamper themselves. The women complimented each other with easy banter while trying on various merchandise.

Martha had nearly paid off the bank loan in just eighteen months. She could see her way clear to running a profitable business with extra cash in the bank for future expansion. True, Martha was working long hours, but it also allowed her younger sisters to earn some money while teaching them valuable lessons about business. Her family was doing well, and Martha felt that many things in her life had settled down.

Mason looked like her little brother, Henry Lee, who was Mama's youngest child. And Mason was smarter than all the other boys his age. Eliza was growing into a young beauty. Sam Crawford still had his business a block away, but Martha had surpassed him with her reputation for haute couture and with her success. She gave him a look of warning whenever they chanced to pass each other.

It was a busy Saturday morning, and Abigail was in the back looking for size 7 shoes like the pair on display that Miss Frances wanted to try on.

"You look like you have lost weight, Abigail," Martha noted.

"Trying to fit into one of your pretty dresses," Abigail always had a smart answer. When they could take a lunch break, she saw that Abigail had brought only a boiled egg and cornbread that looked old and dried out.

"How are things at the farm, Abigail?" Martha inquired.

Never one to mince words, Abigail replied, "Not so good. Papa doesn't seem to have as much get-up-and-go as he used to. James is too busy to see about things at our place. Mama seems overwhelmed with the boys; they always fight each other and try to get out of working."

"What about the hired help?" Martha inquired.

"Sally Ann's brother Johnny has been helping out some. Louis comes occasionally, but he is busy being a preacher now."

Martha frowned. She would check on this next week on her way to the Atlanta Mart.

Chapter 45

MARTHA DISCOVERS TROUBLE ON THE FARM

The following Monday afternoon, Martha was surprised when Bill Billings, the bank president, walked in just before closing time. His brow was furrowed, and he said, "Martha, we've got a problem."

"What's wrong? Was something wrong with my check?"

"No, no. It's not about you. I mean, it is about you, but not the store. It's about your folks."

"My folks?"

"I don't ordinarily do this sort of thing, but, well, I've known you since first grade, and I know how close you are to your family."

"What in the world are you talking about?"

"I don't know what you know about their finances, Martha, but your brother James borrowed money last year to farm. It's not that uncommon for farmers to borrow money to get their crops going."

"For Pete's sake, will you get to the point?" Martha urged.

"Well, the thing is, payment is due. And I have contacted James three times without any payment, and I can't wait much longer."

There was a long, silent pause as Martha's face went from puzzlement to understanding. "What does James say?"

"He says he doesn't have it, but he's working on it. Says the crop didn't turn out so well this year. I wasn't sure anything was even planted when I drove out there. I didn't want to foreclose if...."

"Foreclose! Foreclose? That can't happen. Do you know how long that farm has been in the Dalton family? Generations and generations!"

"Well, I know. That's why I came to see you."

"Look, this is the first I've heard about any of this. Give me three days to find out what is going on. How much is the loan for?"

"I'm afraid I can only give you one more day. It's already overdue. I'm sorry, but there's nothing I can do. I have a Board to report to, you know."

Martha had planned to stop and check on things at the farm next week on her way to the Atlanta Mart, but this couldn't wait. So she called home, told Flossie she would be late, and asked her to stay with the children until their daddy arrived.

As soon as the store closed, Martha drove out to the farm. She hadn't been there in about two weeks and assumed everyone was okay since she hadn't heard otherwise. It was near supper time, and Mama was in the kitchen. Phoebe was setting the table.

"Who is not eating here?" Martha asked when she noticed there were only six plates.

"Papa is in bed. Mama fixes him a tray," offered Phoebe.

"What's wrong with Papa, Mama?"

"All I know is he's poorly." Mama wouldn't look at Martha.

"Have you had the doctor out?"

"No need paying a doctor. He'll be all right in a few days."

Martha opened the bedroom door softly. Her first impression was one of shock; he lay so still. His gaunt face and his soft moan alarmed her. His skin glistened like he'd been working outside on a muggy day. She couldn't tell if he was sleeping or just had his eyes shut. She approached the bed; he looked even worse, close up. Then, as if sensing her presence, he opened his eyes and said, "Huh?" as if she had spoken to him.

"Papa, I didn't know you were sick!"

He worked his tongue around in his dry mouth, wetting his lips before he said, "I wouldn't let Mama tell you. You got enough on your mind with the babies and the store."

"You should have sent word. Of course, I want to know. What is the matter? What hurts?"

"I feel weak, but I'm old. Everything hurts. I'll be all right; just need a little extra rest. Mama and the young'uns are taking good care of me. I'll be up and back to work in no time."

"Papa, who is taking care of the farm business?"

"I have turned all that over to James. I got to where I couldn't keep the books. I forget a lot of things. Is something wrong?"

"I was just wondering who was taking over some of my responsibilities. I always enjoyed helping you with the books."

"Tell me how my grandchildren are," Papa said. Martha could see he was changing the conversation, trying to have a pleasant talk. She stayed on a while longer, then went back to the kitchen.

"Mama, why didn't you tell me about Papa? I know this means things are not getting done on the farm. You should have told me."

"You've got enough to worry about with two stores and two children. You don't need to worry about us. We will make do."

"Mama, you must not let pride get in the way when help is needed. Are you or any of the kids helping James with the books? Who is paying the bills?"

"Papa and James are doing that. I'm leaving that to the menfolk."

Henry Lee spoke up, "I want to help, but James said he didn't need any help."

Martha noted the scarce amount of food on the table and declined Mama's invitation to eat with them. She left and went directly to James' place.

It was getting dusky, and Martha knew James would be out in the fields until daylight was gone. Sally Ann was getting their supper ready while making sure Wyatt was entertained with the wooden toys someone had whittled for him.

Martha had told Sally Ann she could only stay a minute and had to get back home to her family. She went out on the porch and saw James headed toward the house. He was surprised to see her and a little leery of her being here this time of day.

"I won't keep you from your supper, but I need to talk to you for a minute. Walk me out to my car." Martha didn't want Sally Ann to hear their conversation.

"I'll get right to the point. Bill Billings came to see me and told me you haven't made the loan payment. Says the farm is in jeopardy."

"Yeah, well, you can't get blood out of a turnip. The crops haven't been good; there's too much work...." James started in like he had a long list of excuses.

"What about selling off some timber?"

"Who's going to help me fell the trees and load 'em up? Papa's wore out; I'm about wore out too...."

"How much do you owe? Bill wouldn't tell me."

"Payment this year is $300, and I've got $200 saved up. Miriam stays in the store and rings the bell for Drew when someone needs to pump gas. Henry Lee is trying to see to restocking. They're making a little profit."

Martha sighed. "Give me the $200—go get it now. I'll cover the rest. I'm going to pay it tomorrow."

James returned with a humiliated look, carrying an old cigar box. Martha flipped it open to see a disorganized pile of dollar bills.

She looked at him with frustration. "You and I are going to sit down and get some things straight. I will see you on Sunday."

"I work at the sawmill on Sunday."

"Come to my house right after that. And bring the books." With that, Martha got in the car and slammed the door.

Chapter 46

ABIGAIL'S WOE

Phoebe came flying in the back door when school was out. "Did you hear about Dirk Dunaway?" she yelled.

"What about Dirk Dunaway?" Mama answered, and Abigail jerked around on full alert because she hadn't heard from Dirk in quite some time. She feared Phoebe was about to reveal that she and Dirk were planning to elope.

"He was shot and killed this afternoon! Jake shot him because he caught him messing around with Mary Bell!"

"Phoebe, watch your tongue!" Mama said.

"I heard the teacher say that."

Abigail ran over and shook Phoebe. "Phoebe, that's not true. It's not! It can't be!"

"Mrs. Perdue said he was shot, and he was dead."

"He can't be dead. He can't!" Abigail screamed as she collapsed on the floor in great sobs.

"Well, it is true." Phoebe glanced at Mama and said, "What's wrong with her?"

Abigail heard Mama try to explain. "Abigail is upset because it's Doug's brother, and she knows how tragic it is for Doug and all his family. Bless their hearts. But I always knew things would not end well for that boy. Too wild and irresponsible."

The funeral was set for three days hence. Abigail feigned a headache and stayed in bed for the next two days, crying into her pillow until she could cry no more. Then came a message from the Dunaways that they wanted to have Abigail sit with the family at the funeral. She knew everyone assumed she was there to support Doug, and people commented on how emotionally empathetic she seemed to be. Doug was quiet in his grief; Abigail sensed that he knew that her deep grief was not for him.

Weeks passed, and Abigail couldn't shake her sadness. Mama didn't question the fact that Doug didn't come around anymore. After all, one didn't go courting with such a recent death in the family. She overheard Mama telling the younger girls that Abigail's moping around the house was because she was lonesome for Doug. Then Abigail stopped eating and even threw up and remained miserable.

"Why don't you go spend a week with Martha? It would take your mind off your own troubles," Mama suggested. Abigail started crying again.

Abigail knew Martha was worried about her. One night the two were sitting on the guest room bed when Abigail burst out crying. When Martha tried to comfort her, Abigail took a deep breath and said, "I'm in trouble."

"What do you mean?" Abigail saw Martha's expression change like a light bulb went on in her head. "You don't mean you are...."

"Yes, I do mean that! I am ruined. I have disgraced the family! What will I do?"

"I can't believe that. Are you sure? I would never have thought that of Doug."

"It wasn't Doug." Now Martha's face showed raw shock. She was dumbfounded!

"It was Dirk," and Abigail told her older sister everything.

"We were in love. He showed me property he wanted to buy for us. He talked about eloping." Abigail burst into tears. She had been thinking about James' permanent estrangement from the family because of this same thing. She searched Martha's face, hoping to see understanding. Martha didn't waste time sympathizing or chastising Abigail but started discussing sensible options.

"You could go to Lydia in Florida. Have the baby there. Lydia and Walter would probably love to have a baby. No one else would need to ever know."

Abigail felt horror. "I won't give my baby to my sister or anyone. It's all I have of Dirk." Abigail set her jaw to express her firmness.

"Let's go to bed and sleep on it. Tomorrow we will figure out what to do." Then, exhausted, they both called it a night.

For the next few days, Martha and Abigail talked. Finally, Abigail decided the best thing was to go to Florida.

"I want to just disappear from this family. Raise my baby on my own."

"Be realistic. How are you going to support yourself, much less a child?"

"I'll stay with Lydia until I can find a job."

"And who will keep the baby while you work? You don't think Lydia will want to take on that responsibility, do you?"

"I don't know! I don't have all the answers yet!"

"I've found a home for unwed mothers in Rome, Georgia. You could go there, then put the baby up for adoption. I know you don't want to, but that is one option."

"I WILL NOT DO THAT!" Abigail was emphatic.

"Well, face the music and tell Mama. Maybe she will take pity on you and let you stay at home and raise your child."

"Ha! I can't see that happening in a million years. She'd hide the baby and me away, shut up in the back of the house."

They both looked at each other and grinned at the absurdity, but also how characteristic this would be of Mama, who always wanted to put on a front that her life was so perfect. Martha had one more possible solution in mind, but she knew better than to bring it up with Abigail just now.

That week, Elbert was away playing cards with some of his buddies. Martha hadn't even mentioned last night's conversation. Abigail was moving around like a zombie, speaking only when spoken to. She felt numb and exhausted. She and Martha were getting the kids ready for bed when the doorbell rang.

"Get that, Abigail, would you please, while I dry off the baby and put on her pajamas."

"Sure," said Abigail as she dried her hands on her apron. She was stunned to see Doug at the door.

"Well, aren't you going to invite me in?"

"Oh, sorry, yes, of course." Her eyes were downcast, but she moved aside to let him enter. "Martha is in the bathroom with the baby."

She heard Doug say, "It's you I've come to see. I won't beat around the bush. Martha came to see me today and told me everything."

Abigail gasped with embarrassment and looked at him at last, "I'm so sorry."

As if in a fog, Abigail heard Doug say. "What's done is done. I won't say I was totally surprised; I know my brother. I put the blame on him, and I'm sorry you have to pay the consequences." He took her hands in his. "Abigail, you know I love you—have loved you for a long time. I know you care for me and that my brother swept you off your feet. But if you are carrying a Dunaway child, I will love it, him or her, just like it was my very own."

She gasped when Doug dropped to one knee and, with tears in his eyes, said, "Abigail Dalton, will you marry me?" Then, with a dry bit of humor, he said, "And the sooner, the better."

Abigail put her hand over her mouth. This wasn't the joyful proposal she had dreamed of. However, she didn't have to think long to realize it was the best possible solution to her dilemma.

"We will say we eloped just before Dirk died and then decided not to announce it until now." She felt a sense of warmth, wrapped in security, protected. Doug—always reliable. He would take care of her. Everything would be okay.

She knew Doug hoped she would grow to love him like he loved her and she was determined she would try. "I promise I will be a good wife to you, Doug Dunaway."

Chapter 47

LYDIA'S TRAGEDY

L ydia had seen Walter off for his usual trip to Atlanta. It was raining hard, and she added, "Be careful," to her usual goodbye. She would miss him, but she was always glad to have the chance to do just as she pleased—sleep late, eat whenever she felt like it, and go to the movies.

The library was within walking distance of the house, and she had stocked up on some interesting reading material to keep her mind occupied. Fortunately, the library also had books in Braille, so Miss Jenny could entertain herself reading in her room, which allowed Lydia solitude on the veranda. It was still raining, so she settled down with *The Education of Henry Adams* and was just finished with the first chapter when she heard a loud knock at the door. Who would be out in this weather?

She opened the door to find a uniformed officer with a plastic overcoat from head to toe.

"Mrs. Wiggins?"

"Yes," said Lydia hesitantly as she wrapped her arms around her chest. A policeman at the door was never good news; she felt her stomach flutter.

"Ma'am, if I take this wet coat off, may I come in?" She didn't want him to come in, didn't want to hear whatever he had to say. She almost told him to go away.

"Of course, don't worry about the coat. We'll hang it here." Once he had shed his coat, she was jolted into remembering her manners and invited him into the living room. They were both standing, and she noticed he remained close to her. There was a crack of thunder outside.

"Ma'am, I'm afraid I have some bad news. There was an accident about twenty miles from here this morning."

"My husband! Is he all right?"

"I'm sorry to tell you, Ma'am, he didn't make it."

He caught her just as her knees gave way, and she uttered a shrill cry. He took her to the sofa and laid her down. He then noticed an older woman feeling her way along the hallway and heard her cry out, "What is the matter, Lydia?"

He didn't want to scare her but said, "Ma'am, I'm a police officer here to deliver some bad news. Mr. Wiggins was killed this morning in a one-car accident." He thought he would have to catch her too, but the old lady grabbed the handrail and felt for the bench in the hallway, where she sat and put her head in her hands. The officer didn't know if she was the mother or the mother-in-law, but in any case, he now had two fainting women on his hands.

He stayed with them and went to the kitchen to find glasses of water. That's what they always said to do. The water was supposed to keep them from passing out cold. When Lydia could talk, she asked for the details. "It was the rain-slick roads, wasn't it?"

"There will be an investigation, but it appears he lost control of the vehicle. Or else the car hydroplaned. It is completely demolished because it ran off the road and into a tree." Lydia cringed at the graphic detail, but she had wanted to know.

"I'm sure it was instantaneous, so he didn't suffer," the officer said. "Is there someone nearby I can call to stay with you—a relative or a friend?" Lydia looked at him blankly. She tried to speak, but on the first attempt, nothing came out.

"My sister Tabitha and her husband live about two miles from here. I'll get her phone number."

Lydia knew Tabitha would be no help. She would be more emotional than Lydia and not have good sense. But at least she had someone who might help her figure out what to do. She would call Martha as soon as she could muster the strength.

She remembered how it had felt when the doctor told her, "You have a tumor." She felt the same now. All the air was sucked out of her, and she could hardly take the words in. In an instant she knew her life had changed forever.

Chapter 48

MARTHA TO THE RESCUE

Martha took the train down to Jacksonville. It was only a few hours, but she dressed in a suit and sturdy shoes. She believed that respectable people traveled in nice clothes. Leland and Tabitha were there to meet her at the station, and they drove her to Lydia's house. He wasn't much of a conversationalist, and Martha used the ride to think through her plans.

Walter's funeral was tomorrow. Martha had made the arrangements by telephone because Lydia, as usual, seemed helpless. So many disappointments in life, but at least Lydia had had eight good years with Walter. It was the second time Martha had been to her house, and she was again impressed with how well it was kept, thanks to Lula Mae, who had been with Walter's family since he was a young boy.

Martha had arranged to stay for a week. The day after the funeral, she and Lydia went to the lawyer's office to hear the reading of the will. Lydia was left as a well-off widow. Walter had left provisions for his mother in case he would precede her in death. He had specified a comfortable amount for Lula Mae and his cousin, Annie, who had been so kind to his mother. Lydia could not seem to make any decisions and was at a loss as to what to do next. Later that afternoon, back at home, Martha sat her down to try to get Lydia to make some decisions. She knew it was time for a serious discussion.

"Lydia, where do you want to spend the rest of your life—here in Florida in this house or back in Georgia, where you have an abundance of family members to help you?"

"I sure don't want to be back on the farm! And I can't see myself living in a Georgia house alone. I can't manage here in this house without Walter. The money won't last forever, and I can't work with only one kidney. I don't know what will become of me."

"You are stronger than you think, and we will figure something out. What will you do about Miss Jenny? She's your responsibility now. What would Walter want you to do?"

"I can't think about any of that now. I just want to curl up and go to sleep."

Martha sighed and said, "I'm going to have to leave in two days, but I will return in a month. In the meantime, as tough as it is, you need to pack up Walter's things. Maybe Leland can use some of them. Unfortunately, Walter was much taller than James or

Elbert, so that isn't an option. Or give them to the church. You must also think hard about what you want to do with the rest of your life. Try to think about what you have left, not what you have lost. Look at your options for Miss Jenny, and talk to her about what she wants. When I come back, I will help you with your plans."

Lydia was late to pick up Martha at the train station. Martha listened as Lydia explained, "I was at my book club meeting. Today's book discussion was so interesting. It got me thinking about how a book can change a person's life. Mama always chastised me for spending so much time reading, but Walter encouraged me. May God rest his soul."

Just as she had feared, Martha found that Lydia had not made any progress in deciding her future in the intervening month. Walter's things had been packed, but the boxes still sat in the living room. She would call Leland tomorrow and have him pick them up and take them to the church.

"Lydia, you remember we talked about the need for you to make a plan!"

"A plan? A plan for what?"

"A plan for what you are going to do. What are you going to do about Miss Jenny?"

"We never talked about that! You only said I had to pack Walter's clothes. So I did, and I'm too upset to discuss plans! My husband has died and left me here all alone, and there is no plan." Lydia looked at Martha like she was to blame, and she had to fix it.

"My dear sister, the rest of the family wants you close to us in Georgia. You have some money, but you are right—it may not last your whole lifetime, so you need a way to earn a living," Martha said as she sat Lydia down at her kitchen table. Lula Mae had made a pitcher of iced tea, but Lydia hadn't offered her any. Martha poured them each a glass.

"Have you paid Lula Mae? I suspect Walter did it weekly."

Lydia looked at her, puzzled. "No, I haven't."

Martha was exasperated. She made a mental note to check all the bills later.

Neighbors had brought food soon after Walter died, but there was not much in the house now. Martha had called Annie and asked her to pick up some essentials.

"I don't know how I can earn a living! You know I only have one kidney, Martha. I can't work!"

"I know, I know, but there are other things you can do to have an income. For example, you can take in boarders. Lots of people do it. I found a property back home that I think is ideal for you, and you can afford it. It is on the south side of town but still close enough that the family can get to you in a hurry if needed.

"The house is like two big apartments with a hall running down the middle. You can live on one side, put Miss Jenny in a bedroom across the hall, and still have plenty of room to have another boarder who could pay you monthly rent. It has a well and a septic tank with one bathroom at the end of the hall that everyone could share. It is a large property; if it were laid out just right, you could advertise for people coming down from the north during winter to park their trailers there.

"The house is right on the highway from Atlanta and an ideal spot for people on their way to Florida. Our brothers can help you set up the trailer park. It would take hardly any effort on your part. There's already an outhouse there for the trailer park. There's also a small store on the property."

"Oh no. No store. I couldn't stand on my feet in a store all day," Lydia replied.

"Well, you could stock it with necessities and open it only a few hours a day. There's also a henhouse there, and fresh eggs always sell. It's about three acres, so you'd have plenty of space for your privacy, and yet it is not too far from town. You'd be near family who could help you, but not too close to anybody."

Without so much as a "thank you" to her sister, Lydia said, "I guess I better go tell Miss Jenny to start packing."

"It looks like I'm going to have to make another trip to Florida to help Lydia settle things and get moved back to Georgia."

"Martha," said Elbert, "I worry about you. You take on too much. All your siblings and even your mother expect you to solve their problems. And you have a full life with the children, your and my stores...."

"Without you, Elbert, I couldn't do it. Sometimes I wonder, 'Am I just meddling? Should I be judging what the right thing for others to do is? Do I step in too early to help, as if they are incapable or incompetent? Am I interfering rather than helping?"

"Martha, you and I are each the oldest child in our families. I think we have always felt it is up to us to see that everyone is okay. And if we didn't act and things turned out badly, we'd feel guilty. So, I guess I'm saying you are doing the correct thing, and I will support you. I'll also watch you and tell you if I think you are overexerting yourself. Go to Florida with my blessing."

Within six months and with Martha's guiding her all the way, Lydia was settled in the house. She had found a boarder, a lovely older lady who had lost all her family. It was a double bonus for Lydia; not only was Miss Matilda a steady income, but she also became a companion to Miss Jenny.

Martha monitored the income for the first few months. The trailer park was a big success. Besides the northern travelers, a gypsy fortune teller parked her trailer there permanently, and the store was doing good business, too. The two older ladies were getting along well. Flossie helped find someone to clean the house and cook for Lydia.

Elbert told Martha, "Lydia always has lots of stories to tell about the comings and goings of the trailer customers. She's even talking about writing a book. But she seems to have settled into her new life. Another family crisis handled, Martha!"

Chapter 49

JAMES AND LYDIA DISCUSS THE FARM

James knew that Papa had never recovered his full strength but continued to work as hard as he could. His drinking had gotten worse. The farm was in bad shape. James was stressed and still bitter because he was only paid at the hired help wage level. He was doing practically everything himself but admitted he was doing a half-hearted job because he had his own place to worry about. With his extra work at the sawmill, there just wasn't enough time to go around.

He didn't intend to kill himself, carrying the entire load on the family farm. Mama was outside more, trying to help out, and all of the girls left at home had jobs around the farm. Mama was worn out from having eleven children, but at least the last two had been boys, who could do more physical work.

Drew was now fourteen; he had trouble hearing ever since he had been kicked in the head by a mule when he was six years old. He wasn't very ambitious either. On the other hand, Henry Lee was the golden boy—glib of tongue, full of personality, a charmer with the girls, even at the young age of eleven.

Neither boy seemed to heed James' instructions; there were too many years' difference in their ages to feel like he had any big-brother authority over them. Papa could make them help out, but he seemed absent-minded. Clearly, Henry Lee didn't like the farm and considered it beneath him. Farming was okay with Drew, but he didn't keep up with what needed to be done unless somebody told him step-by-step what to do. All this depressed James, and he told Lydia so on her weekly visit. James wasn't sure if Lydia came because she was lonely, wanted to make sure she didn't miss any family gossip, or if she felt a kinship with him since the two of them seemed to have all the family's bad luck.

"I know Papa isn't carrying his load anymore. What are you going to do when you can't keep up?" she had asked James.

"He hasn't been carrying his load for years. And I already can't keep up. And those sorry brothers of mine are no help. Papa sees about the livestock, and the hired help do as they please. Harvesting the crops has become a joke. I think he needs to turn the fields into a pasture and forget about planting cotton and corn next year."

"Will they have enough income?"

"Mama has a small garden, enough to feed them still at home. Papa can kill a hog every now and then and butcher a cow. Timber is a good source of income, and the woods have a-plenty."

"Does Martha know how bad things are?" Lydia asked.

"I don't know what the hell Martha knows. It's really none of her business. That's what's wrong with this family. Too many people into each other's business. Telling everybody what they ought to be doing." He didn't care if his bitterness showed.

"What's Martha ever done to you, James?"

"Nothing, that's the problem. Martha should have confronted Mama and Papa about how they treated me and how they still treat Sally Ann and me. She's the oldest, and they both listen to her. It took me three years to get together enough lumber to build this house, and our woods are bursting with trees!" he continued.

"You have a right to be angry, James. I know how stubborn Mama can be and Papa is too sweet to buck her."

"I don't think I'd call it *sweet.*"

Chapter 50

JAMES' CHANGING CIRCUMSTANCES

It was late in the afternoon the next Sunday when James saw Lydia drive into the yard in the fancy automobile Walter had bought her a year before he died.

"Sally Ann, here's Lydia showing off her big car again," he said.

The special treat on Sunday was to go for a ride and get an ice cream cone in Batesville. His son Wyatt now had a baby brother, Willard, and they both loved ice cream. It was good for Sally Ann to get out. Lydia always timed her visit for when James got home from the sawmill. She liked hearing all the family gossip from James' perspective because she felt a kinship with his cynicism.

Being the philosopher that she was, Lydia always had an opinion about what was going to happen, mostly doom and gloom. They had discussed how rapidly Papa's health seemed to be deteriorating.

Just then, there was a furious rapping on the door. Henry Lee stood there completely out of breath from running.

"Come quick, it's Papa." He turned and started running back.

"Henry Lee, get in my car. Quickly! Let's go," Lydia said to James.

When they arrived at the house, they all got out of the car and ran. All the commotion seemed to be at the barn, so that's where they headed. James got in the barn first but stopped short. Lydia brushed past him. Papa didn't usually drink until late at night. James felt fear and a weird tinge of revenge.

She acts as if she knows all about sick people with her one year of nurses' training.

James stood back as Lydia knelt down on the straw outside the stalls where Papa had apparently collapsed. She felt for Papa's pulse.

Lydia looked up. "Nothing."

James could see Papa's lips were blue, and his face was in a grimace; his legs were twisted at an odd angle. He had his right hand over his chest.

"He may have had a heart attack or a stroke, or maybe both. He's gone." Lydia announced. James felt a curious mix of emotions, and he didn't move.

There was an unearthly cry in the barn as Mama dropped to her knees. Drew stared, mute and motionless. Henry Lee reached out to Mama and tried to comfort her.

"Oh, my poor darling John. What will become of us?" Mama wailed.

Indeed, what will become of you, James thought? It was uncanny that he and Lydia had recently been talking about the changes that were sure to come for the farm. In a flash, he saw his circumstances had changed. He certainly couldn't take on the responsibility of Mama and the kids left at home. They would have to step up and take care of themselves just as he had had to do when his family threw him to the wolves at the age of seventeen. And no more taking only ten percent of the timber sale after he did all the work of cutting the timber and hauling it to the sawmill. From now on, it would be a fifty-fifty split. And no one needed to know because it was payback time.

People said the funeral was a lovely service and tribute to a fine, upstanding pillar of the community. As the oldest son, James stood beside Mama with Sally Ann on his other side. He knew Mama would have to bite her tongue not to complain about the line-up as others would know the oldest son and his wife were now the new head of the family.

Martha had brought black dresses for all the women. Mama had on a hat and a veil which she kept lifting to wipe her eyes. Beulah Baptist Church was full. Mama and Martha had planned the service, with three of Papa's favorite hymns: *How Great Thou Art*, *In the Garden* and *The Old Rugged Cross*. Pastor Edward gave a beautiful eulogy and prayer. They all walked to the adjacent cemetery to the Dalton plot for the burial service.

After the funeral, James and Sally Ann were at the house when people from the church and from all over the county brought food for Miss Betts and the family. James tried to make himself scarce. These were the "Christian" people who had snubbed Sally Ann years ago, and he had not forgotten it. If anyone asked, working at the sawmill on Sundays had given him an excuse not to be seen in the church.

Martha had asked Sally Ann to help her sisters in the kitchen. The little ones had their own table and thought this was a party, being with all their cousins. Martha pulled James aside and said, "We have to talk. Help Mama make some decisions."

"The decisions have been made. She can't continue to farm. I can't do the work by myself. We probably need to sell some of the land. No need in letting it lay fallow."

"We'll have a family meeting tonight after all the guests have left," Martha instructed.

James dreaded this, but it had to be done. He decided he would let Mama have her say, but from now on, he was running things.

"I won't leave my house." Mama had put her foot down. "Drew and Henry Lee are old enough to do farm work; James can teach them all they don't already know. The girls can help out more. We will manage."

The girls remained silent, not used to having any say in matters anyway. Mama continued, "And I won't hear of selling any land that has been in the Dalton family for generations. We are saving it to give you children when you want to put your homes on this property."

Everyone was silent.

James then laid out his plan since he had anticipated this day. "Mama and the kids should stay right here. We won't plant a fall crop because we don't have the manpower to plant or harvest."

Martha responded, "Then you won't have to borrow money from the bank."

"What will we do with all the land?" Drew asked. "Seems a waste to let it lie fallow."

"We'll turn it into pasture for the livestock. A lot less work," James said. "Drew, you and Henry Lee will have to take care of them. I'll work with you for a month or so until I'm sure you can handle it."

Henry Lee stared blankly at James. He had not said a word.

"What about the store?" Lydia asked.

"Nobody can run the store, so close it down," James said firmly.

"I suppose that is the practical idea," Martha said.

"I can take the store contents," Lydia said.

"Or better yet, Elbert can buy the stock for Hall's Grocery and give Mama some ready cash," Martha spoke up.

"The boys can help expand the garden, and Mama, you and the girls can tend it from there. You all should be able to keep one milk cow and enough chickens for eggs. That should feed you," James said with authority.

"Mama, do you think we can do all that?" Phoebe and Miriam were all crouched together.

"Yes, we can. And we will," Henry Lee answered and patted Mama on the knee.

"One more thing," James added, "Papa paid me wages, but since we are reducing the farm, that won't be needed. Instead, I'll spend more time at the sawmill and be in charge of cutting and selling the timber. Louis, Drew and Henry Lee can help. I'll give Mama the proceeds after each sale."

Martha looked concerned and said, "James and Mama, I know Papa set up the books to record the crop, livestock and timber income. And record the bills that were paid. I can help with the bookkeeping if you want me to."

"I think I can manage that," James said dryly. As the oldest son, the place was his now, and he didn't want anybody interfering. Mama would have to depend on him.

Chapter 51

MARTHA FINDS MORE TROUBLE ON THE FARM

Three months later, Martha got a call from a friend at the county tax office, alerting her that the annual property taxes on the farm had not been paid. Martha had a sinking feeling but reassured her friend she would take care of it as soon as possible. That afternoon she rode out to the farm. She planned to talk to Mama first. "Mama, who is paying the farm's property taxes, you or James?"

"I am. I'm going to do it as soon as I have enough money."

"That's not the way it works. You have to pay it on time, and it was due at the end of last year."

"Well, I can't pay what I don't have."

"But James just sold several loads of timber. What was your share?"

"That wasn't enough."

Martha frowned. Something was obviously not right. "Let me see the books."

"We don't have any books. James just brings me the cash that is my share."

Martha couldn't believe what she was hearing. James must have the books. And Mama should have had adequate funds to pay the taxes. Something was clearly wrong.

Martha couldn't decide if it was carelessness or a deliberate attempt to cheat Mama of her share of the timber. She preferred not to think the worst of her brother, but things had to change. She had enough experience in the business world to know things had to be set up and accounted for properly—no matter how much you trusted those involved in your business.

She bought a ledger, sat Mama and James down, and explained the bookkeeping system they would use from now on. She asked James to bring the timber receipts home and keep them in the back of the ledger. James would get some help cutting the timber and get a 40-60 split. And she announced she would go over it with them on a quarterly basis.

Mama should have enough income to maintain the farm and pay the bills. Of course, they would have to be frugal, but they should be able to manage. James didn't say a word; he just sat there and listened.

Then, when Martha was ready to leave, he walked with her to the car, and she knew he wanted to tell her something out of Mama's earshot.

"If you think I have time for some fancy bookkeeping, you are sadly mistaken, Martha," his face was red, and his fists were clenched. "I bring her the receipts; if she loses them, it's not my fault."

"She says you don't bring them to her every time."

"Well, she's getting old, and she doesn't remember everything. It's been a 50-50 split, and I paid Louis to help me. If the split is going to change, Louis' pay will come out of her portion."

"I think you should split Louis' pay between you."

"I tell you what I'll do. We're cutting tomorrow. When I take a load in, I'll use Mama's share to pay the taxes, get that burden out of the way," James proposed.

"Will she have enough for food and what the other kids need?"

He nodded yes, but Martha wasn't reassured. And she wasn't sure he'd abide by the change of split. She also wasn't sure Mama would keep the books correctly.

As she drove home, Martha was conflicted. She knew James needed money with a growing family. She wanted Sally Ann to have a good life; she had been such a good friend to Martha. If James fudged a little, should she simply look the other way?

Chapter 52

LYDIA BECOMES POPULAR

L ydia spent most of her day writing. Her book was coming along nicely. But writing was a solitary pastime, and she was lonesome. Although she had spent much time alone while married to Walter, she still missed his companionship. She seemed to have all the bad luck in the family. The house was a lot of trouble to maintain. When something broke, she usually left it broken and just made do. When Martha or another sibling visited and noticed the problem, they would take action and see that things were fixed.

The trailer park was taking care of itself without too much maintenance required from her. Lydia usually had one or two guests there all the time. Some stayed for weeks, and others stayed until they got the urge to go somewhere else. The gypsy fortune teller had plenty of customers, people who were traveling to Florida and saw her roadside sign.

Lydia didn't open the store on a regular basis anymore and didn't keep it stocked. It was too much trouble. When her sisters came, they brought a few groceries and maybe some clothes they didn't want anymore. Some people might call that charity, but she wasn't too proud to accept it. In fact, she was amused that her siblings showed such sympathy for her. As she watched her siblings working hard— Martha at the store, James and the boys on the farm, and the younger girls having jobs on the farm and in town—Lydia gloated over her uncomplicated life.

One Saturday morning, she was sitting under the shade tree out in the garden on the side of the house. The flowers Drew had planted had done well. It was probably the farmer in him. The gardenia smell was heavy in the air. That was one of her favorite flowers. The shrub did well in the full sun. The wisteria was winding through the tree branches, its vine heavy with purple flowers. There was a gentle breeze that ruffled her hair which she had pinned up to make her neck cooler. She was reading a book and enjoying the morning quiet when a strange car drove into the yard. Lydia sat still, watching to see who would emerge. The driver honked the horn, but she didn't move. Whoever it was would have to come to her.

When the driver emerged, Lydia stood up and cried, "Lily Jane! I can't believe it's you!" Lily Jane made her way to Lydia, and after hugs and kisses,

Lily Jane sat down beside her old friend on the garden bench.

"I heard about what happened to Walter, and I'm so sorry. What has it been? Almost a year? Al and I just moved back here from Savannah. He will take over for Daddy and be a peanut farmer." Lydia knew that Lily Jane had married Al soon after finishing nursing school. But Lydia had lost track of her after moving to Florida.

They had a good visit about the old nursing school days, Lily Jane updating Lydia on several of their classmates. Lily Jane had worked as a registered nurse in a Savannah hospital but wasn't sure what she would do now that they had moved back home. Maybe she'd help Al get established in the farming business.

As Lily Jane got ready to leave, she said, "Lydia, I think you are depressed. You've had some sad events in your life, but you know what they say, '*Behind every cloud, there's a silver lining.*"

"Not behind my cloud."

"Look on the bright side. You are an independent woman; you do as you please all day. You are financially secure if you never lift a finger again. Your family sees about you. You are still young enough to start in a new direction in life."

Lily Jane continued, "You know, Richard is still single. Maybe you two should get together again."

Lydia wasn't sure how she felt about that. She rather liked her life of being a semi-invalid without very much responsibility.

"You need some fun, Lydia. You are too young to wither away. And Richard is handy and could help you out with this big place. What you need is a boyfriend. Or should I say a gentleman friend?" Lily Jane laughed.

Lydia looked at her friend out of the corner of her eye.

Lily Jane's eyes lighted up. "I know! Let's have a party. Al and I will bring Richard over on Saturday night. We'll bring the booze."

"I see you still got the devil in you," Lydia said and they both laughed.

It didn't take long for word to get out that Lydia's home was the place to party on Saturday night. It was a "Bring Your Own Bottle" affair. She bought a fancy Victrola. The house was big enough, but often the party spilled over outside. Men began to drop by and bring Lydia presents. She found herself being popular for the first time in her life and she was enjoying it. She reminded all of them that she only had one kidney, so she never cooked a meal for them or showed any sign of reciprocity for their thoughtfulness.

Richard had never married. He lived in a small cabin near a creek and earned a living doing odd jobs. He became a regular at Lydia's house, showing up on Saturday mornings. He was good at fixing things. Although he wasn't overly ambitious, things were looking better around the place.

And he made Lydia laugh. He was always joking and teasing her. He was frisky too, and Lydia had to admit she liked that. She had been too long without a man. Sometimes he spent the night. *Well, she couldn't very well send him home after so much drink.* She didn't think anyone knew and if they did, it was none of their business. Miss Jenny couldn't see and had also become very hard of hearing. So if she sensed anything, she never said.

It was not until she had a visit from Martha that she realized everyone knew more than she thought. Martha always gives advice on the importance of a good reputation. *That and a dime would buy you a cup of coffee*, Lydia mouthed to herself.

Chapter 53

MARTHA AND HER FAMILY GET A SURPRISE

Martha counted the number of adults squeezed around Mama's dining room table. Everyone had brought dishes. All the girls were good cooks. There was ham, potato salad, deviled eggs, biscuits, green beans, pimento cheese sandwiches, pineapple sandwiches, and fried chicken.

Mama asked Elbert to say grace, and the meal began. The sweet iced tea glistened like cinnamon as Abigail proudly served everyone from her new Jewel Tea pitcher. There would be apple and pecan pie for dessert. All her siblings and their spouses had come.

Abigail could hear the squealing from the other room at the children's table. They were bolder in misbehaving since their parents were out of sight. The adults were engaged in lively chatter, happy to see each other and catch up on the news. Mama looked festive in her red dress that had come from the boutique. She had plaited her white hair and coiled it on top of her head, like a real Mrs. Santa Claus, complete with a white apron.

Mama had even applied the blush that Phoebe had brought her. She smiled at her brood as she entered with a pan of biscuits to replenish the empty platter. Martha noted her mama was more stooped now but still insisted on having Christmas dinner at her house every year.

How much longer could she live alone and be independent, Martha wondered. Mama had learned some lessons the hard way since Papa died. The farm business had changed, and finances were tougher.

Mama and Papa's dreams for the farm had turned out so differently than they had hoped. They had wanted the land to be an estate which would be kept in the family and passed on to many future generations. The large family was part of the plan. Many hands were needed to run the farm, store and timber business. All the girls loathed the chores required by a farm.

Had Mama inadvertently passed on her sense of entitlement based on her own pampered childhood in the town's parsonage? She wanted her daughters to be Southern ladies, not husky farm girls. And Papa had always treated Mama like a queen, not expecting her to do outdoor jobs. And he had been soft on the girls too.

Was he following Mama's leanings or was he not a good farm manager to not hold the girls accountable? Or was it the alcohol? Did it override his judgment and start the farm on its downward trajectory? Or maybe James got subconscious satisfaction in seeing the farm's demise as he withdrew his wholehearted support in response to how he was treated.

Certainly, there had been no spirit of teamwork or sense of meaning in jobs well done. There was no consideration of what jobs appealed to whom, just rigid assignments roughly based on age. On the other hand, maybe it was not so different from other farm families. They seemed to think that hard work never hurt anyone and that parents had a duty to teach each child responsibility.

Well, it had backfired. All but James had fled the farm as soon as halfway feasible. Nevertheless, family members had found new paths—paths more suitable to their own preferences. Their lives had turned out so much more interesting and varied than if the eleven children had each been given a plot of land and remained on the Dalton land.

Martha was glad she had been able to spare Mama from knowing some of the problems she and her siblings had experienced. For example, Martha had never shared her ordeal at the department store with anyone except Sally Ann, who had never mentioned it since. Then there was James, with his hand in the till and his bitter resentment of how

Mama and Papa had treated him and Sally Ann. Mama had finally accepted them; James had forgiven, but not forgotten. Mama never knew that Martha had rescued them financially more than once.

Lydia was sweet to Mama, but didn't want her to know all her business. She was a published author now and somewhat of a celebrity in the family. And Martha hoped Mama would never hear the rumors about Lydia's partying with alcohol flowing freely while entertaining friends at all hours of the night.

Abigail and Doug seemed happy enough. The younger child, Robert, was just like Doug in looks and temperament, but the oldest one, Jack, was handsome and charismatic. He was clearly the favored son in Abigail's eyes.

The other siblings all had their stories, too. It was a tale of life in a big family.

Martha remembered all those years ago when she wanted to get away from this farm. She had gotten away, but not very far. And maybe the chaos was not from all the work to be done on a farm but rather from the people in her family—these same people sitting around this table. *You can't get away from your family*, she thought and sighed. Somehow they had all survived and remained close.

Martha's musings were interrupted when Mama stood up and tapped on the tea glass with her spoon.

"I invited you all here because I have some news." Mama had everyone's attention. "As you know, it's been ten years since Papa died. I loved him and miss him dearly. But things change, and life moves on."

"What do you mean, Mama?" Phoebe blurted out. Her impatience was showing.

Mama cleared her throat. "Well, I wanted to tell you that I am going to get married again to Reverend Phineas Edward. You know, he lost his wife three years ago. He asked me last week, and I said yes. I will move into the parsonage at Beulah, and Drew can live in this house."

Phoebe was the first one to regain her voice. "But Mama...."

"Well, I always wanted a preacher in the family. And none of you girls would humor me and marry one. I couldn't make any of my boys into a preacher. So, I'm going to be the one to get us a preacher in the family!"

ABOUT THE AUTHOR

Patsy Lee's grandparents lived on farms in South Georgia. But most of their descendants preferred city life, a fact which seemed peculiar to a child who loved the ambiance of farm life as an occasional visitor. When she was a preteen, Patsy's parents sent her alone by bus for a 13-mile trip every Saturday to her step-grandfather's country store, where she was to "help out." They would come up on Sunday for a big dinner, visit with the family, and then take her home. In the store, she would count out Johnny cakes, those giant brown sugar cookies, for the customers enjoying the fragrance from the big glass jar. She would also restock shelves, sweep, and do other odd jobs. But mostly, she listened and learned some things about life.

The store was a place for connecting and visiting for these disparate country neighbors. And let's face it—sharing gossip about others was the news everyone wanted to hear, just as it is today. Patsy recalls, "If I appeared to be listening, the conversation was often guarded and subtle, which only set my imagination to work filling in the unspoken parts."

Many of these stories remained in her memory for years, and she often thought what a good book they might make. So after retiring, Patsy joined a local writing club at the public library and started the process of weaving an integrated whole out of these embellished snippets. However, any resemblance to actual characters—living or dead—is strictly in the overactive mind of the reader!

She chose to use her maiden and childhood name as the author, as she felt like that little girl from South Georgia in sharing these stories with you.